Ch

C000040195

Book 1
Anxiety Superpower Series

by

Dean Stott

Chloe, and all of the other books in the *Anxiety Superpower series* are not a form of therapy, nor should they be construed as a substitute for professional medical or mental health advice. The content in them is for entertainment purposes only. They are not intended to diagnose or treat you in any way.

Reading any or all of the books in the series, and interacting with the author or DLC in any way, does not constitute a therapist/client or counsellor/client relationship.

Please always consult your own medical and mental health provider, if you have any questions about your health or well-being, or are feeling unwell.

ISBN: 978-1-7397478-1-7

Download the dlcanxiety app for free
https://www.dlcanxiety.com/the-dlc-anxiety-app

Website link: www.dlcanxiety.com
Instagram: www.instagram.com/dlcanxiety
Facebook: www.facebook.com/dlcanxiety

Contents

Prologue

She had run from the car, a Volkswagen Polo, and was watching now from the safety of the trees. Not caring that it had started to snow again. Or that she was alone, and miles from anywhere in the middle of the night.

As soon as the car screeched to a halt, she had thrown the passenger door open, Slamming it quickly behind her, before she started to run. Almost at the same time as the driver was pulling away.

The ice on the road soon slid the small car into the opposite lane. Spinning it once for good effect before an articulated lorry, travelling faster than it ought to have been on a winter night, collided with it.

In no time at all the grinding and crunching of metal on metal became the broken wreck of the car, and the night was silent again. Except for her screams as she stared at what she had done.

Not noticing the shoulder bag, lying on the road. Thrown from the back seat of the vehicle when the impact occurred. The driver of the car didn't survive.

CHAPTER 1

A New Job For Chloe

"**P**ut the kettle on, Hannah!" Mark said, knowing that she wouldn't want to. It was difficult enough getting her to answer the phone, and greet the clients politely.

"You could do it sometimes. I don't know why it always has to be me," she said, with a loud groan. Glaring at him from under a mess of spiky hair which didn't suit her round face. Before she filled the kettle with as much noise and drama as she could manage, and switched it on. Banging the three mugs, and a single china cup, onto the tray to emphasise the point.

Undeterred, and clearly enjoying the banter, Mark began to complain about the last coffee she had made for him. Telling her sternly that he hoped this one would be a lot better. Hannah was about to say what she usually did that he should make his own when Mr Jones, the manager, came out of his small office at the back.

"Hannah Simpson, we have had this discussion before! I don't want to have to tell you again. It's part of your job as an administrative assistant, and receptionist, to make the tea. Not Mark's, nor mine. Mark Fowler is an estate agent. Not an admin assistant." Before adding miserably that he had already been waiting for ten minutes for his own tea, and sincerely hoped it wouldn't take her much longer.

"Sorry, Mr Jones. I'll bring it through to you when the kettle has boiled," Hannah said, automatically, and without meaning it. Turning back to Mark when she saw the manager close his door, to whisper that it still wouldn't hurt him to do it sometimes.

The cold draught when the front door opened interrupted any further discussion that might have taken place between them. A tall, willowy woman in her mid-twenties walked through it. The highlights in her auburn hair shone under the electric light which Sarah Poulton, the senior estate agent, had put on when she arrived first. Deciding that a dark morning in early December wouldn't encourage any of them to get a lot of work done and Chloe Burton, the latest addition to the team, was already proving to be a distraction. At least for Mark. His saturnine eyes were exploring every inch of her. As she stood waiting on four inch heeled boots, for someone to show her to her desk.

"Hi, Everyone," Chloe said, sounding reasonably confident, and pleasant. Nevertheless once she realised that all of them were staring at her, and Mark's eyes had found a path through her clothes to her skin, she patted her hair quickly. Checking that none of the strands had gone astray. She had spent some time last night practising different styles, and trying on several possible outfits before reaching a decision on what to wear. Jack hadn't been much help. Not that she expected him to be. He was often lost in a world of his own, and her lips widened into a smile as she thought of him.

Sarah, who looked to be in her mid-forties, came forward and took Chloe's umbrella from her to put in the bucket next to the front door. "Good morning, and welcome! Do you want to sit at the spare desk next to mine?" She said, gesturing to it, before turning to Mark and Hannah. Both of whom were watching what happened with interest.

"You have already met Chloe when she came for her interview, so I won't do the introductions again. Let's just make her feel very welcome. Hannah, can you sort out a drink for Chloe, please?" Realising that she was unlikely to do this without being prompted, and she was right.

Hannah turned to Chloe and said, without smiling, "tea or coffee?"

"Black coffee. No milk or sugar, and can I have a cup, if there's a spare one?" Chloe smiled sweetly at Hannah whom she saw was overweight, and looked to be around twenty. Confident that what she had asked for would be done.

Meanwhile Mark was becoming even more excited. He liked a woman who knew exactly what she wanted. He had already decided that he would ask Chloe for a date, as soon as he could. Just in case she left after a couple of weeks, like her predecessor had done. Unable to cope any longer with creepy Mr Jones, as Hannah had so elegantly put it. Mark refused to accept any suggestion that he had played a part in this, and Hannah hadn't for once mentioned his bad behaviour so far as women were concerned. She was only too happy that Karen had left.

He was still watching Chloe who obviously looked after herself properly. Unlike Hannah. He couldn't help making the comparison now. Although he had also subjected her to his charm when he arrived in the office two years ago. He would invite Chloe to the gym where he went every morning without fail, and as if Sarah knew what was going through his mind about skimpy leotards, she spoke sharply to him. "Give Hannah a hand with the drinks, Mark. Now! Then have a look at those new sales particulars I put on your desk. The properties are in the newspaper today, and on Zoopla, so we may get some enquiries. Despite the bad weather. I'd like Hannah and you to deal with them while I show Chloe what we do, and help her get started."

Mark smiled at Chloe then. Using the special smile he practised in front of the mirror. Showing her that there weren't any hard feelings. Even though Sarah was telling him what to do. He said, in a caring tone of voice, "you can always come to me if you have any problems, Chloe. Anything at all." Before his heart sank so far inside his chest, that it felt all over again like the dumb bell falling onto his foot earlier that morning. When he had cried out in pain, the other gym goers whom he knew didn't particularly like him, couldn't stop sniggering about it.

He still didn't know how he had done it. Not putting the dumb bell back in the rack properly, after doing his bicep curls. At least Chloe hadn't seen what happened, he had been thinking with relief. Until he noticed she was wearing a wedding ring. Okay, things might be a bit more complicated, but that had never stopped him before. He would have to play it a bit differently. That was all. Just let the Mark Fowler charm work its magic.

Chloe's cheeks had by this time turned a little red, and she was clearly about to say something which would knock Mark back when Sarah interrupted what he was trying to start. Passing a cup of black coffee to Chloe, and the super hero mug to him. Asking her to sit down. After she had put her coat in the cupboard in the corner.

When Hannah was behind the reception desk again after taking Mr Jones his tea, and Mark was reading the sales particulars online, Sarah said in a low voice, "please don't mind them! They do this every time there's someone new, and have almost the same argument about the tea and coffee every day. It always ends the same way, with Hannah making it, and although Mark does think a lot of himself he is harmless. You'll see."

"That's fine, Sarah. I really don't mind, but thank you for saying it. I try not to let things bother me, and I want to make a go of the job. The more help I can get the better. Including from Mark, and Hannah."

Sarah looked at Chloe's flushed cheeks, and wondered if she meant what she had said. She did look a little flustered, but thought anyone would on their first day at Jenkins & Co, the only estate agency in Mappingham. "That's good. You aren't in the least like your predecessor. Karen was very anxious. She obviously couldn't cope with, let's just say, the strong characters in this office. If you want to shadow me this week, Chloe, I'll show you exactly what to do. I know that you don't have any previous experience of this sort of work, but you'll soon get the hang of it. I am always here, if you have any questions. Please don't hesitate to ask."

Chloe smiled at Sarah gratefully, before turning to the computer and asking her about the property on the screen. Who would be likely to buy it, and did Sarah think the price was reasonable? Not intending to waste any time whatsoever in knowing what to say to any awkward clients she might come across. Her father had suggested that she try to find out what made them tick, as soon as possible, to use this information to her advantage. He had been thinking about the extra commission she could earn on the sales her colleagues weren't able to make.

Meanwhile Hannah had left her desk to join Mark at the photocopier. Not having had any customers so far that morning, presumably because of the snow. It was hardly ideal for viewing properties, and most of the other enquiries could be dealt with by email or telephone. They only had a couple of completions before Christmas when the keys would be left with them, and they weren't until Friday. For Hannah, and to a lesser extent Mark, it was the ideal opportunity to waste even more time than usual. Both of them were however disappointed they could only do this with each other. They would have much preferred Karen's replacement to be more like them, but it was only a regional office. Mr Jones also didn't need any other staff except Betty, the cleaner, who came in when they had closed for the night. To empty the bins and hoover the carpet. Even if they had still been at work, neither of them would have been particularly interested in her.

"Never mind. You can't win them all," Hannah said, digging Mark in the ribs with her pen. Wondering how hard she could push without him shouting out, and attracting attention to them. She nodded quickly in the direction of Mr Jones' door which he had opened. He was standing perfectly still staring at Chloe. "Same old story," she added, with a grin as she headed back to her desk. Thankfully neither of them bothered her now. Not being good enough for Mr Jones she thought, and as Mark was a bit of a social climber, the same probably went for him. Although she had told him early on that she was a lesbian, and not interested in him.

Hannah almost burst out laughing, and just managed to stop herself in time. She still wasn't sure whether or not he had believed it. He could be such a fool! Anyway it did the trick. It would be interesting to see what happened with Chloe, as she was very attractive Hannah thought begrudgingly. Already jealous of Chloe's Zara dress which she had seen online, and couldn't afford to buy. Those boots too weren't off the stall in the market, like hers had been. No wonder she seemed so full of herself, and could probably deal with a bit of sexual harassment in her stride.

Nevertheless if you wanted to get on, you had to make sure people liked you, and Hannah had decided a long time ago that not being friendly with the manager was the real reason she hadn't been promoted. Although this was far from the truth, and similarly that Mr Jones was guilty of any harassment. She had conveniently forgotten that she didn't actually do a lot of work. How would their more influential clients regard someone like her? The question had been asked by Mr Jones in a confidential conversation with Sarah. Even though Sarah didn't have any influence whatsoever on who was or wasn't given a wage rise, or promoted.

Hannah smirked. All of them were only here now because they couldn't get a job anywhere else. Time would tell, as it had done with Karen. Chloe would probably find out how to do everything, then put it on her curriculum vitae that she had experience of working in an estate agents' office. Only to get another job soon after that. Anyway she was probably married to someone rich. That was it, and being here was just to get her some pocket money for clothes and make up. All the things Hannah wanted but couldn't have, because Mr Jones didn't pay her enough for everything she did. She realised then how much she already hated Chloe Burton!

A rich husband was the answer. All of her friends wanted one, and she didn't even have a boyfriend any more. Not after Jay gave her the push a few weeks ago. Hannah's eyes filled with tears, and she swivelled her chair around quickly. So that she was sitting with her back to the room, and could wipe her eyes without anyone noticing.

"Are you alright, Hannah," Chloe said, catching her in the act. "Is there anything I can do to help?"

"No!" Hannah managed to say it in such a way as if Chloe would be the last person on earth she would ask.

Chloe however didn't react to her unfriendly behaviour, and changed the subject quickly. Adopting what Hannah regarded as an authoritative voice, and which Mark still had to master. "Sarah asked me to bring these over.

Can you enter the clients' data on the system please?"
Chloe said, as her eyes bore into Hannah's. Making it quite
clear that she didn't expect any arguments, or trouble from
her, if she was asked to do something. Before she walked
back to her own desk, to start work again on the other
tasks she had been given.

Hannah glanced at the papers and soon pushed them to
one side, before opening the TikTok app on her phone.
Holding it under her desk so that no one else could see
what she was doing. Although it wasn't as good watching
videos, with the sound turned off. What she couldn't see
was that Chloe's heart was now racing, and beating inside
her chest like a bomb. Or that she felt completely alone.
Her father had only been able to help her up to a point,
with how she could go about doing the job. Not how to
deal with the people she would be working with.

Hannah also didn't know that Chloe couldn't wait to go
outside at lunchtime, to get away from them. Whilst
somehow becoming the best estate agent in the British
Isles, who earned the most commission. Knowing that
there would undoubtedly be far worse to come. Since once
she started to make more sales than Mark, who had been
glancing at her for most of the morning, he wouldn't take
the assault on his ego at all well.

Chloe sighed quietly to herself. There was absolutely
nothing she could do about any of it. Apart from carry on,
and brazen it out. She could hardly complain about either
of them when she had only been at work for less than a
morning. Mr Jones seemed a bit odd too, the way he had
stared at her. It wouldn't surprise her if he was hiding

something. He had been weighing her up, she could tell. Sarah was the only one who was genuinely nice. She would have to be very careful not to upset her or that really would be the end of it. However she might appear, Chloe didn't really have a lot of confidence in herself. Did she? The small voice inside her head reminded her, also of how useless she could be when she let down her guard.

She had promised her father, and Jack, that she would do her best to become a good estate agent and she had absolutely no intention of failing. Even if it was a far cry from doing admin work in London, after leaving University with an English degree, and the florist's job she had last. But what if she really couldn't do it? The small voice inside her head insisted. No! That wasn't going to happen. She wouldn't let it. As long as she kept her head, nothing could possibly go wrong. Could it?

CHAPTER 2

Married Life

"How was it?" Jack shouted from the living room where he was painting. While Chloe took off her ankle boots, before walking barefoot across the carpet to plant a kiss on his lips. Which ended up in him pulling her onto his lap, and kissing her deeply. "Mmm, I have been waiting to do that," he said, brushing his lips playfully across hers to tease her. "Did you miss me?"

"Of course I did," she said, trying to stand up but he was too quick. Kissing her again before she could move. Slowly, and lovingly.

Afterwards on her way to the kitchen, and feeling a little guilty, she said over her shoulder, "I'll make it up to you later, Jack. I promise." Before pouring herself a large glass of wine from the open bottle in the fridge.

"Hey, where's mine?" He said, in surprise. When he saw just how large her own drink was, and that she hadn't brought one for him.

"Sorry, I forgot, but it's really nice wine!" Chloe grinned, running her tongue slowly around the rim of the glass, then drinking from it enticingly.

"Oh that's great, isn't it. Here I am slaving over my latest masterpiece trying to get the perfect balance between light and dark, also the blue just right, while my wife forgets all about me. Not only that, I have even put something in the oven for supper."

"I just need a few minutes, Jack, that's all. I could never forget about you," Chloe said, softly. Putting a glass of wine on the coffee table in front of him. Next to his paints, and the watercolour he had been working on. She ran her fingers slowly along his thigh before she sat down in the chair opposite.

Jack stared at her. Almost unable to believe that she had just done that, and this was the same woman he had married, a few weeks ago. She used to be so shy. Yet had started now to instigate sex more than he did. Seemingly insatiable at times. Although he wasn't about to tell her this in case it put her off. He was enjoying himself too much to risk it.

He had a lot to be thankful for. Chloe's father had bought the apartment for them in Mappingham, as a wedding present. It was a small town sixty miles from London, with a river and a mediaeval castle, along with lots of history. After an initial day trip he had desperately wanted to move here, to pursue his career as a landscape artist and painter. The gallery owner in London, who sold a couple of his paintings, had promised to give him an exhibition of his own when he had enough canvases ready. Sam had called him a new and exciting talent, and Chloe had been thrilled for him. He couldn't believe sometimes just how much he loved her, but he did.

He really liked, and admired her father. Steve Wilson had done everything he could over the years, to keep his family from falling apart. Chloe's mother had died of cancer when Chloe was eight years old. Her brother, Harry, was the eldest. There was also a sister, Natalie, both of whom were a few years older than Chloe. It couldn't have been easy for any of them, Jack thought for the umpteenth time. Whilst Chloe and her father had understandably grown very close. It was even better than that, Jack thought. He got on well with all of them, and felt very much a part of the Wilson family who had welcomed him with open arms.

"It's a lovely painting," Chloe said, staring at it while she drank the rest of her wine. "Are you going to send it to Sam for the exhibition?"

"Yes, I think so. I have been retouching some of the sky. I didn't think it looked quite right. Of course it would have been better if I could have done it outside, but that obviously wasn't possible today. I think I have got it right though. Has it stopped snowing?"

"No! Good thing that we don't live too far from the office," Chloe said, pulling her long legs up under her body, to sit more comfortably.

Jack watched her doing it. Wondering what exactly she had in mind for later. "I thought you were keeping your new dress for Christmas Day," he said, not really thinking about what he was saying. "When we go to your Dad's for lunch. Sorry, I meant the restaurant he has booked."

"I changed my mind, Jack. That's all. I wanted to look nice for my first day at work. Don't forget I don't have any experience, and everyone else does. So the least I could do was try to look my best," Chloe said, irritably.

She wasn't about to tell him that Hannah had barely spoken to her, from jealousy she assumed. Or that Mark was a walking nightmare. She had to do this for all of them, and Dad had asked her a couple of days ago to make Mum proud which she had promised to do. Not start worrying again that she would fail. When the job had been advertised it said no experience or qualifications were necessary, and that training would be given. Chloe felt the familiar rush of adrenaline coursing through her veins the more determined she became. Jack had told her she could smash this! Once she got into it, and she had to believe him. Maybe it had been a bit over the top to wear the Zara dress today, and she would definitely make sure she wore her sensible boots tomorrow. Her feet were aching tonight, and she could easily have fallen over. Perhaps it had been a little foolish to wear heels in the snow, and ice?

"Hey, I understand. I was just asking, and you don't need to try so hard," Jack said, interrupting her thoughts. "You look amazing in whatever you wear. Or don't! How was it anyway, at work?" He asked again, beginning to wonder now why she hadn't already told him.

"It was fine. Just a lot to learn, and some of the people are a bit difficult, but nothing I can't handle," Chloe said, firmly.

"What do you mean difficult?" Jack said, with concern. Not intending to let anyone bother her.

"It was nothing really, and if you don't mind I'd rather not talk about it. I'm too tired. What's for supper?" She replied, changing the subject to one she knew Jack liked. He was a real foodie. Having backpacked around Italy in his gap year, he knew a lot about Italian food and wine, also how to cook it.

"Yes, okay. Sorry. I've done a lasagne. There's some ciabatta too, and a green salad. I was going to get a tiramisu, but thought you wouldn't want it." Jack's eyes lit up at the thought of the rich sauce he had cooked earlier for the lasagne, and he had of course made his own pasta.

"No, I wouldn't have wanted a pudding. I'm not really very hungry," Chloe added, as Jack looked at her again with concern.

"Chloe, all this watching your weight is fine and I hate to sound like I'm telling you what to do, but I think you need to eat a bit more."

"Please don't start again, Jack. I eat more than enough, and my clothes don't fit or look good on, if I get too fat. You know that," Chloe said, refusing to be deterred.

"No, Chloe, I don't," he said, brusquely. "You lost a lot of weight for the wedding and I don't think you should lose any more. You look beautiful now, but it's not healthy to be too thin."

Chloe burst out laughing. "If I still had a mother, Jack, I am sure she would sound exactly like you. Although Dad used to keep an eye on what I was eating after Mum died, then Grandma," she said, suddenly becoming more serious as she remembered the past. Fleeting images of a woman she had known as her mother until she was eight years old, and the grandmother who had also died not long afterwards.

"I understand how hard this is for you, Chloe. Starting a new job and moving from London. I hope you know how much I appreciate what you have done for me. Supporting us both until I can get myself known as a painter. It's been a godsend for me, coming here. Surrounded by countryside and nature. There were only so many paintings of Hyde Park I could do, and Sam has promised me an exhibition as soon as I have enough finished canvases to show at the gallery. It won't take me long. When I am famous you won't have to work at all," he said, hopefully. Realising deep down that there was also the possibility this might not happen, or take many years to come to fruition, but that was life! So much could change over time, and he couldn't let this opportunity of becoming a professional artist pass him by.

"Chloe, you know how much I love you. When I look back now, that day we hit it off at Uni seemed like the beginning of my life. I have never felt like that about anyone else," he said, looking at her with love in his eyes.

"Nor me, Jack!" Chloe said, smiling. "My own art student, two years older than me, and more often than not covered in oil paints. Someone who would pick up one of my poetry books to start reading Byron, Shelley, or Yeats to me. I couldn't believe it at first. Or that we could be different in so many ways, and also very happy together. You were always the life and soul of the party, Jack. While I was the shy, introverted, girl with a book under her nose. I loved doing that English literature course, and going to the art galleries in London with you. Seeing you filled with so much passion for them, and the men and women who had painted the old masterpieces a long time ago. Of course I wanted to help you follow in their footsteps.

I don't have much chance of writing the next Nobel prize book, but I can see myself married to the next great landscape painter, Jack Burton. It even sounds right."

Chloe paused for breath, and to look at him properly. Jack was wearing the jumper she loved to cuddle up to. Despite being scruffy and covered in paint, he still looked amazing in it. Incredibly sexy too! His broad shoulders helped, she thought, before realising that he was waiting for her to say something else. "Please stop worrying about me, Jack. I'll be fine at work, and I will try to eat a bit more. I promised Dad too, that I would be alright. I don't intend to let either of you down. Especially after what you have both done for me," she said, kissing Jack tenderly.

He was prevented from saying or doing anything else by the sound of his mobile phone ringing. When Harry's name appeared on the screen, and he said that it was her brother, Chloe told him to answer it. Harry was in the Navy, and rarely called Jack. So it must be important. "Mate, how are you doing?" Jack said, in the way he usually answered the phone.

Watching her husband's facial expression change, to become more serious, Chloe began gesturing to him to tell her what Harry was saying. While Jack held his free hand up, to show her that he needed to listen. "I don't know what to say, except that I'm very sorry. Yes, I understand, and of course I'll tell her. You take care of yourself, and give our love to Natalie. I'm glad that she is okay. Keep in touch, Bro'."

By the time Jack had ended the call Chloe was unable to wait any longer for him to tell her what had happened.

While he groaned inwardly when he looked at her. Trying his best not to show how deeply Harry's news had affected him, and the last thing in the world he wanted to do was hurt her. "Let's sit on the settee, Chloe. I want to put my arms around you, and I don't really know how to tell you this," he said, sadly, and worried about how she would react. Despite her protests he refused to say any more until they were sitting next to each other. "There's been an accident, Chloe. It's your father… He's dead."

"No, Jack! That's not funny. Saying something like that. I know when you are lying, and Dad's not dead. I spoke to him yesterday. We are seeing him on Christmas day," Chloe said, pulling herself from under his arm, and turning to face him. "You are always teasing me about being a Daddy's girl, but this is too bad. You have to stop being jealous about it, and me being able to twist him around my little finger. He's my Dad, and I love you too. You should know that by now!"

Jack was feeling completely out of his depth by this time. Starting to doubt Harry's decision that he should tell Chloe. Simply because he was her husband, and was there with her, Harry would have been the best one to do it, but he had to call Natalie back. He was at the Navy base in Portsmouth, and Jack hadn't realised Chloe's sister was on her own. She had taken the news badly. So not knowing how else to handle it, he repeated what Harry had told him. That their father had been killed in a car accident.

Chloe screamed at him then, still trying to stop him from telling lies. She carried on insisting that it wasn't true, but after he refused to back down, she eventually asked him calmly how it had happened.

Jack held both of her hands inside his own, as he told her that he didn't know anything else. Other than that there had been a car accident, and her father was driving. "Steve didn't make it, Chloe. I am so sorry, my darling."

Jack's arms were around her then, holding her tightly. While Chloe's world turned upside down, and she fainted.

CHAPTER 3

Going To Dad's Funeral

It was no longer snowing but bitterly cold, as Chloe and Jack waited with the other mourners in the churchyard. Both of them lost in their own thoughts.

Jack was focusing on the yew trees that had been there for many years, and was looking at them as an artist would. Along with some of the graves which, according to a cursory glance at the headstones, went back to the mid-eighteen hundreds. The church was in contrast reasonably modern, and had been renovated a few years ago. There was little else to look at, and use as a distraction from how he felt. Only a small group of people had gathered together on the path. Apart from immediate family, and a few friends of the deceased, an elderly great aunt was the only other remaining member of the family and she wasn't well enough to travel.

Chloe's attention was focused on Deborah Slater, or Debs, as her father had started to call her affectionately. Of course she was there! She had been seeing Dad for the last eight months, and did seem to be upset by his sudden death, Chloe thought reluctantly. Although she didn't particularly like the woman, and had assumed the feeling was mutual, Chloe felt now that it was her duty to include her as much as possible. Given that Dad had started to treat her as if she was one of the family. Despite this not being true and she could never replace Mum. Nevertheless, Chloe had only managed so far to say a quick hello to her. Acknowledging her presence, that was all.

Chloe glanced at her sister, Natalie, standing next to her who seemed now to have a tissue permanently attached to her face. Wiping away tears or a runny nose. She sighed, inwardly. Keeping her face straight. Not wishing anyone else to know her true feelings. Nat was so good natured, and kind. Exactly like Dad, gullible. She had also thought there wasn't any harm in Deborah going out with him, if it made them both happy, and it clearly did. Chloe was however still secretly waiting to be convinced of her good intentions. A forty year old divorcee probably wouldn't have lasted in the long run. Once she found out that Steve Wilson didn't have a lot of cash to spare. Irrespective of how many boxes of chocolates, and flowers had come her way.

Chloe frowned. At least all of that would stop now, she thought. She couldn't imagine Dad would have left Debs anything in his will, but whatever happened, she would keep her word. Nothing was going to stop her from being the success he had wanted her to be, or to prevent her from keeping her promise to him. So even if she didn't feel quite herself at the moment, it was important that she didn't let it show and carried on dealing with everything. It was all she had left now of Dad. There was no way in the world she would let anyone take it from her.

Chloe was dressed from head to foot in black, which she wouldn't usually do. When Jack had tried to persuade her gently, to add a little colour to her outfit she had refused, and the tone in her voice was enough to tell him that she wasn't going to change her mind. All of her underwear was black too. In the end Jack had decided to leave her alone. To let her deal with the tragedy how she wanted, or needed to. Not knowing that Chloe didn't want anything to distract her, even choosing different colours. So intent was she of keeping her father's memory alive through the promise she had made to him, she wasn't prepared to risk doing anything which might become a betrayal of this.

Chloe didn't realise that Jack was still feeling out of his depth. Unable to believe something as tragic as his father-in-law's death had happened when he had only been married a few weeks. Jack hadn't known his own father, and he wasn't close to his mother. She had little to say about it. Only to give Chloe time, and he had come to the conclusion that she was simply getting herself through the funeral in the only way she knew how. He wouldn't be at all surprised if Chloe fell apart later when it was all over. Harry had been inclined to agree with him. When they had the opportunity to discuss Natalie, and her briefly. Sharing a sense of family responsibility between them. Jack had told Harry that from the little Chloe had said, she was still unable to believe she wouldn't see her father again. Or that he was in truth being buried today.

Jack also didn't know that Chloe thought everything seemed to be happening in a blur. As if she was only a spectator at the church that morning, and none of it was real, He had told her that Harry arranged the burial, and service, with Natalie. He had asked her if she wanted to be involved in making the arrangements. Chloe remembered shrugging her shoulders when he had said it. What did it matter when it wasn't real? Harry was only doing it because Dad had appointed him as executor in his will, so it was his job to make the arrangements. He no doubt thought that keeping Natalie occupied would stop her from crying so much. Whilst Chloe had her promise to keep to their father, which he wouldn't want to stop her from doing. No! It was only right that she carry on as she had been doing. To do well at work, and in life generally. To make Mum proud, as she had agreed to, and undoubtedly him too.

It had been just over a week since the accident, and the coffin had stayed closed. They hadn't been able to see their father again, as the crash had been too bad. The Doctor said that he would have died outright so not felt anything, but he had severe burns and multiple broken limbs. The driver of the lorry had also been killed. The police thought that he had fallen asleep while driving his vehicle. Allowing it to cross the central reservation on the M25, and collide with Dad's car travelling in the fast lane. Miraculously no one else had been hurt, the police officer had said. As if this made it acceptable for everyone to be telling her that her father had died. Why couldn't it have been someone else? She had already lost too many people she loved, Chloe thought.

Although she still felt numb, it must be cold out here. At least the others seemed to be feeling it. Pulling scarfs, and coats closer around their bodies. Checking that their hats were pulled down as far as they could be, presumably to keep out the wind, but they didn't really care. Did they, about Dad? Jack was still holding her hand. He hadn't let go of it for very long since the night Harry called, and Natalie was still standing next to them. Crying softly. While the church bell tolled. Every time it rang the sound resonated loudly through Chloe. After it had happened she could hear everything much louder now. Even if someone had dropped a pin on the other side of the room, she thought that she would be able to hear it.

They were almost ready to carry the coffin inside. Jack pulled her hand gently. Intending for them to follow her father on the last part of his journey. Whilst his mother clung to his other arm. Chloe wanted to scream at her. That she didn't have any right to be there. She hadn't seen Chloe's father since the wedding, and barely spoke to Chloe or him even then. Not being satisfied with her son's choice of bride. Much preferring her friend's daughter who was a doctor, but of course none of that mattered now. She would speak to her mother-in-law after the service. Along with Deborah. She had to say thank you to them both for coming. It was what Dad would have expected her to do.

Chloe grabbed Natalie's hand, and held it tightly. She would be strong, to help her sister get through this. Harry too. They might be older than her, but she had promised Dad that she would be strong and she was. Chloe Burton, nee Wilson. She noticed then the pale sunlight breaking through the cloud, and shining momentarily on the coffin which the undertakers' men were holding on their shoulders. Not that Dad would weigh a lot, she thought. Not now, after the accident. She squeezed Natalie's hand and removed her other one from inside Jack's, so that she could hug her sister. Making Natalie sob even harder.

Harry meanwhile glanced at Jack, then Chloe, and they both knew what the other was thinking. What was wrong with her? She hadn't cried since that first night, and only briefly then. Whilst the way she was acting now was bizarre. Even Jack's mother was crying quietly beside him, and all he could do was shake his head in response to Harry's unspoken question. Maybe grief would hit her harder later on, he thought again. Not knowing what else to think. He wished with all of his heart it had been otherwise. He would miss his father-in-law being in their lives, and he couldn't bear to see Chloe like this.

Jack glanced along the path in front of the church. Judging by the long faces around him, Steven Wilson had been well liked. Harry was doing his best now to talk quietly to as many of the mourners as he could, before they followed the coffin inside the church, and Chloe appeared to be about to join him. Until Jack put a hand on her arm quickly, to intervene. Insisting that she stay with Natalie instead, as her sister needed her the most. Without saying it, he also thought that Chloe would benefit from being with her.

When Chloe looked back on that morning, everything remained a blur. It seemed like no time at all before she was standing next to Jack, with Natalie and Harry, at the graveside when the Rector said a final prayer. Each of them threw a small handful of earth onto the coffin. Jack was holding Chloe's hand again as she did it, and he added his own. While Harry held Natalie's hand. That was all. Chloe knew that Dad wasn't there.

Then somehow it was all over. The hymns, the Rector's voice, and Harry talking about Dad. So that Chloe found herself in the room Harry had hired above the Green Man public house. Just down the road from the church. Those who had been at the service were packed inside it, and she remembered afterwards that her skin felt too sore to be touched. So she hoped that no one would. Jack had whispered to her that her voice had become too loud, and brittle. Although she didn't notice it. She talked a lot about anything and everything, to the people who had joined them for a drink, and a sandwich. She could tell that Jack was feeling uncomfortable when he kept looking at the ground, as she carried on talking quickly. He didn't seem to realise that she had to. How could she keep her promise to Dad that she would be okay, if she stopped talking?

She was saying something now about not doing a reading in the church, and could easily have done. She knew exactly what Dad would have liked her to say. Harry and Jack looked pointedly at each other again. Both of them felt very uncomfortable. The old Chloe didn't push herself forward like this, and Jack put his arm around her shoulders. "Hey! Everyone knows how much you loved him, Chloe," he said, quietly. "There's no need to worry. It's fine."

When Jack went to the toilet and Harry became distracted by an old friend of his father's, he failed to keep an eye on her. So she took the opportunity to talk to Deborah. Saying how surprised she was that she hadn't been in the car with her father on the night of the accident. Although she was of course pleased that she hadn't been, Chloe had added hastily.

"There was a last minute change of plan," Deborah said, looking confused, and not really knowing what to make of the question. Given that she believed Chloe hadn't approved of her relationship with her father. "Otherwise I would have been. Poor Steve, I shall never forget him." Her eyes filled with tears again, and Chloe thought she would suffocate when Deborah hugged her. Pulling away when she felt unable to breathe. "Oh, I'm so sorry. I didn't mean anything by that," Deborah said, quickly. Seeing the look of alarm on Chloe's face.

"Why didn't you stop him?" Chloe said, angrily. Just as Jack came back.

He interrupted the conversation straight away, to ask her if she wanted another drink. Taking her hand again, and gently pulling her to the bar to stand beside him. While they waited to be served he kissed her forehead, and told her how proud he was of her. He knew that her father would have been too. Chloe leaned into him for a few seconds. He thought she was finally going to talk about Steve's death when the barman asked what they would like to drink, and the moment was gone.

Later that day once they were at home again, it was as if nothing had happened, and Chloe was getting her clothes ready for work the next morning. Jack came into the bedroom to ask her what she was doing. "You aren't ready to go back, Chloe. You shouldn't have gone in last week. Mr Jones understood. He said you could take as long as you needed to."

"But I'm alright, Jack. I want to go to work," she replied, folding up the scarf she had decided not to wear.

"Please, Chloe, listen to me. All of this has been a huge shock. I want you to think about yourself for once, Take some time, to at least get used to what's happened."

"What do you mean, Jack? I'll never be used to the fact that I can't pick up the phone and speak to my father. I loved Dad dearly. I also promised him when I was a little girl that I would be strong enough to carry on. Whatever else might happen after my mother died, and that's what I have to do," she said, using her hand to push him to one side. "Please get out of the way. I want to finish this, and I need to find my other bag. It's somewhere at the back of the wardrobe, I think."

Jack grabbed her arm. "Chloe, promise me you'll speak to the doctor tomorrow, if you won't listen to me. I'll get you an emergency appointment, and go with you. I won't come inside, if you don't want me to, but at least see what he thinks about you going back."

She looked at him, and shook her head slowly. "I don't know what you imagine he'll be able to do. The medical profession still can't bring people back from the dead, Jack."

"For Heaven's sake, Chloe! I am talking about you. Not your Dad. If you can't understand how I am feeling, that I am seriously worried about you, then please just do it for me," he said, desperately.

Something in the tone of his voice must have got through to her, and she nodded once. Even smiled at him. "Alright, if we can get an emergency appointment early, so that I can go straight into work afterwards. That's the only way I'll go!"

For the first time since they were married, Jack slept with his back turned to her that night. Utterly out of his depth. He was certain by now that this version of Chloe wasn't the same woman he had married a few weeks ago. Was her behaviour down to grief, or something else? She had changed as soon as she started her new job. Becoming more dominant, and the way her moods changed was peculiar. All of this new found confidence wasn't at all like her. It had to be grief, he supposed. She was really close to her father, and understandably so. Bereavement took a lot of getting over, from the little he knew of it, and she had been through a lot. At least she was seeing the doctor tomorrow. He was the one to ask, but the thought continued to niggle. Although it had to be grief, the more he thought about it there had been some changes in her before her father's death? None of it made any sense.

Jack realised then that it wasn't right for him to behave like this. They had agreed a long time ago that they wouldn't go to sleep feeling annoyed, or fed up with each other, and here he was sleeping in a grump. He turned around slowly, to put his arms around Chloe. Kissing her softly, and he whispered goodnight.

It wasn't long however before the same thoughts returned to his mind. Does someone who has just buried their father want to go back to work the following day? Jack felt so confused, that he lay awake for a long time trying to find the answer. Eventually falling asleep when it was nearly dawn, still none the wiser.

CHAPTER 4

An Appointment
With Doctor Symes

"Chloe, are you sure you don't want me to go in with you?" Jack said, again. Changing direction slightly this time, by adding, "I won't say anything. I promise. I'll just be there, if you need me."

He wished that he had been able to speak to the doctor yesterday, as he tried several times to do, but Dr Symes had been too busy to take his call. He couldn't help but be worried that Chloe wouldn't tell him how she was really feeling, and that he would be taken in by the bright and breezy attitude she had adopted this morning. As if she didn't have a care in the world.

"Jack, this has to stop!" Chloe replied, turning her head to glare at him, before she relented and sighed heavily instead. "How many more times do I have to say it, so that you'll believe me? I know you are only trying to help, but simply because we are married doesn't mean I can't do things by myself. How on earth do you think I'm going to manage at work, if I can't talk to other people by myself? I won't have Sarah in the office holding my hand forever, and you can't go everywhere with me," she said, matter of factly. Not bothering to lower her voice when an elderly lady came into the waiting room, and began looking curiously at them.

Jack however coughed in embarrassment. Not feeling quite as confident as Chloe appeared to be, and looked. She was immaculately dressed in a dark blue suit. With the pearl buttons at the top of her pale blue shirt left undone, to give a tantalising glimpse of what was underneath the jacket. She had taken off her long, wool coat when they came into the building. While he still had his fleece on, and scarf wrapped around his neck. She didn't seem for some reason to be feeling the cold. Even when they had been outside at her father's funeral, which was another surprise. She usually complained about not being able to get warm. Wearing several woollens at a time from the huge collection of clothes in her wardrobe. Also hugging a hot water bottle at home, which she regularly refilled.

Jack frowned. He hadn't been able to put his finger on it until this morning. Chloe seemed to be too perfectly in control, and determined to get on with her life, which he hadn't expected at all. Especially after Steve's death. It was weird, and she still hadn't cried. Her make-up was immaculate too. So she hadn't shed a few tears when he had been in the bathroom. Neither had her hand slipped, the way it often did when she was putting on mascara. At least she wasn't dressed all in black like yesterday, and had used the smokey grey, eye shadow he liked. Giving her eyes a mysterious, and definitely come to bed look.

Jack almost smiled then. If he was being honest with himself, he was biassed. He was completely lost in her.

Her eyes usually looked like that to him. Whether or not she used eye shadow. He couldn't help hoping the men in the office wouldn't think the same. From the little she had said he didn't think she rated the manager very highly. He did sound like an old dinosaur, but she hadn't really talked about the other estate agent, Mark. He would try to find out more about him tonight. It wasn't a question of him not trusting her, which as far as he was concerned, he did implicitly. Only that he knew what men were like, and Chloe was stunning.

"Hey, no worries, if that's what you want to do. I was only trying to help," he said, attempting to diffuse the situation. Now that they had an audience and Chloe would be called in shortly to see the doctor. He patted her hand gently with his own, by way of a peace offering.

Chloe gave him a half-smile in acknowledgement of the gesture. She had to remember that it must be hard for Jack too, she thought. Given time he would surely be able to see that she was only doing what she needed to. Being strong! The same as she had told her father on many occasions in the past she could be. When he had worried about her. She ought to be able to cope much better now with bereavement and what life might throw at her, since she was no longer a child. Which was exactly what she was doing. She consoled herself with this thought when her name was called by the receptionist, and she left Jack behind in the waiting room. To walk down the corridor on her own.

Neither Chloe nor Jack had met Dr Symes. Having only recently moved to the area. Nevertheless she could feel a boost of energy running through her as she walked into his room. She could tell straight away that he was tired. He looked stressed. He was rubbing his face. His room was very untidy. With three mugs of what looked to be half-drunk coffee scattered around, and a plate with a half-eaten bacon roll on the desk.

Not having to think about what she was doing, Chloe took control of the situation when she was only half-way through the door. Introducing herself in what she regarded as her professional manner. Holding out her hand confidently, for him to shake. Then launching into her reason for the visit, which she attributed to Jack's concern and anxiety about her well being. Explaining that there was actually nothing wrong with her. She didn't need medication, a sick note, or any other help and she had to apologise for wasting the doctor's valuable time.

Unable to stop talking, she said then that her father had died recently, but he was a very down to earth man. He had dealt with the bereavement of her mother by going back to work after only a couple of days, which he had spent with his young family. Once her grandmother had stepped in to take care of them. Even though she wouldn't necessarily have passed on this piece of information, Chloe didn't know that Steven Wilson had little choice in the matter. Things had been very different years ago, and he worked for an unsympathetic boss who told him his job would be on the line if he didn't get back to work.

However she also said, before Dr Symes had spoken a word, that she had recently started work at the local estate agents. She was in the middle of her training at Jenkins & Co. Everyone had been nice to her, and very kind, so she didn't want to let them down. This really wasn't a good time for her to be absent. It was an excellent career move, with a higher salary. Reiterating then that she was perfectly fine.

Dr Symes had by this time removed his spectacles to wipe them clean. Using the cloth from inside the case where they were kept. Only half listening to the young woman who had sat herself down, and was rambling on about him not giving her a sickness note. She apparently didn't want one. Although that had been the point of her being given an emergency appointment!

Groaning inwardly, he looked impatiently at Chloe and noticed her flushed cheeks. Her pupils appeared to be dilated, if he wasn't mistaken, and she was talking nineteen to the dozen. Despite her protestation to the contrary and from this cursory examination, she was most likely suffering from anxiety and the effects of the recent bereavement. Meaning that she did need some help. Which was only natural, if the funeral had been yesterday, and she was as close to her father as he assumed she had been.

Chloe was also correct in her assumption that Dr Symes was busy, and tired too. Nevertheless doing what he believed would be best he said, kindly, "I am inclined to agree with your husband, Jack. I think you said that was his name. I'll give you a sickness note for two weeks, to be on the safe side. It'll give you some time to sort out how you are feeling."

He paused to emphasise the point. "Don't forget too, that you will both be in the process of adjusting to being newly married. All of this will have affected Jack. It's understandable. Maybe he needs the reassurance of you being at home with him for a little longer. I can also put you on the list for some counselling sessions. It may be a good idea to have them. They help people get through difficult times like this. Take Jack with you when you go to the meetings," he suggested.

Chloe noticed Dr Symes scrutinising her face, as he waited for her reply. Although he was at the same time clearly anxious to get back to the paperwork on his desk, which he was moving about with his right hand. Instead of giving her his full attention, she thought. That should make it easier to persuade him to leave her to her own devices. Even more so when the telephone on the desk rang at that very moment, and Dr Symes picked up the receiver. Chloe could hear the receptionist reminding him that his next three appointments were already in the waiting room, and he was running late. Causing a smile to cross her lips, and disappear before he had the chance to see it.

Dr Symes was frowning when he put down the phone, and turned back to her. Not bothering to write the sickness note he had intended to. The receptionist had reminded him of the more serious injuries he would have to deal with today, despite how exhausted he was. Being called out in the middle of last night, to examine a patient who died before the ambulance arrived. Chloe Burton was the least of his worries, and she did seem to have everything in hand. A highly competent young lady, by the looks of her. She was attractive too, he thought fleetingly. Maybe she didn't really get on that well with her father, and didn't like to admit it. There was no knowing what was really behind all of this, without exploring it further with her, and an emergency appointment only gave him enough time to make a quick assessment of the situation.

"Well, I'll leave it to you then, shall I? If you insist you don't need a sickness note. You know where I am if anything changes, Chloe, and I will put you on the list for counselling. Just in case," he said, forcing himself to smile encouragingly at her. Whilst she got up quickly and said thank you, before closing the door behind her.

Dr Symes looked briefly at it. Feeling guilty that he didn't have enough time to talk to her properly, but that was how it was now. He finished his bacon roll quickly, and drank the rest of his latest mug of cold coffee, before picking up the phone to ask the receptionist to send the next patient in.

Jack left the waiting room when he heard the next name on Dr Symes' list being called out, and he walked outside with Chloe. Waiting for her to tell him what had happened. She looked elated, so everything must have gone well.

"It was as I thought, Jack. I'm fine. There's no need for you to worry about me. The doctor agreed that I didn't need any more time off work," she said, triumphantly.

"What about counselling?" Jack asked, unable to keep the irritation from his voice. Wondering what Chloe had actually said to the doctor, or more likely, didn't tell him.

Delighted then that she had something else which might appease him, and stop him from being quite so persistent, she told him that her name was on the waiting list for counselling. Giving Jack the opportunity to query why the doctor had done this. He must have thought she needed help after all, which Chloe denied vehemently.

Saying it was only done as a precaution in case anything changed, which it wouldn't. She kissed Jack's lips, and said that she would see him later.

As she was about to turn away he grabbed her arm, and said, "Chloe, let me walk with you to the office. I can go back to the flat that way." Realising that there was little point in arguing any further with her about her decision to go back to work so soon, it was now a case of seeing what happened next, and still being there for her if she needed him.

Her reply came far too quickly, he thought later. "Thank you, Jack, but it isn't far. I don't want to give any of them the wrong impression about why I am late. They might not believe I've been to see the doctor, if I am with you."

Jack couldn't quite see the logic in this. Only how determined she was to do everything on her own now, and be in control. The truth of the matter was he had an ulterior motive in offering to walk to the office with her. At least that way, anyone who might be interested would see that they were definitely a couple. They had talked about jealousy when they first started dating, and she was so shy back then it had never been an issue for either of them. Now however he wasn't so sure, because of the way she was behaving. He didn't like it. Something was definitely wrong. People didn't suddenly change like this! He was wondering now how long she would be able to keep it up. Without heading for a burn out, or breakdown. He assumed that either of these could be the next step, although he didn't really know. Maybe he needed help too, he thought.

"Alright then. If you are sure," he said, brusquely, and without knowing what else to do he kissed her cold cheek. "I'll see you later." He watched her walk away from him then, for the second time that morning.

Chloe didn't look back to wave. Already thinking that she would be able to get to the office much quicker in the boots she was wearing. It shouldn't take her very long at all. It might even be before nine o'clock when she arrived. She had got her own way too with Doctor Symes, and she could smooth things over with Jack tonight. Play up to his ruffled pride. She knew by now what he liked doing most of all, and how to make him happy.

The training she was receiving from Sarah had gone well, and she had been able to concentrate. Despite what Jack might think. It also hadn't stopped her from feeling numb or thinking about her father, but it made it much easier that she was doing what he had wanted for her. Jack didn't understand. That was all, but he would in time. He would realise that what she was doing was for the best. She certainly didn't begrudge being the sole breadwinner. Jack's life would change dramatically if she lost her current salary, to earn what she assumed Hannah did. That would be ridiculous, and Dad was right, as he had been all along throughout her life. This was by far the best way. Jack had a good chance of making a success of his painting.

Chloe pulled her scarf a little tighter around her neck, which she believed was the best way to wear it, and began to walk faster. With the intention of arriving even earlier than she had originally thought she could.

CHAPTER 5

Thrown In At The Deep End

Chloe looked at her computer screen. Breathing a sigh of relief that they seemed to have stopped watching her, at least for the time being, and she would be able to sit quietly for a few minutes at her desk. Everyone stared when she opened the front door a few minutes before nine o'clock, and walked into the office. Waiting for her to break the silence. She had said good morning as brightly as she could, to no one in particular. Trying to appear calm, and collected, despite still being anxious that she would be the last to arrive. As the sea of faces turned to a brightly coloured blur in front of her eyes, and it had taken until now to appear more normal.

Neither Mr Jones nor Sarah had said anything about her being last, and she wasn't technically late. So she had turned on her computer without any further explanation of her appointment with Dr Symes, and carried on studying the files she had been given to read. Not having any emails to reply to on the system. Since she was still waiting to be given some property files of her own, and have her first clients to manage.

Her breathing was however erratic, and it felt unpleasant. She hoped that stopping for a few minutes would help to slow it down a little. Blaming Hannah's thick, black, coffee for it. She had put the kettle on at eleven o'clock as usual, and banged the cup down onto Chloe's desk. So that the liquid slopped over the rim onto her notepad. Chloe had stopped herself from complaining. Realising just in time that this was exactly what Hannah was hoping she would do. She seemed to thrive on confrontation.

There was something very wrong with the receptionist this morning, Chloe thought. She had barely responded when she said hello to her, which was fine if that was how she wanted to be, but it was as if she no longer cared about her job. She was surly, and abrupt on the telephone. Impatient too. Muttering under her breath about how nothing seemed to be going right. That she had, well and truly, had enough. No one else seemed to notice her bad manners, and ignored her. Causing Chloe to come to the conclusion that this must be how she usually behaved, but which still didn't make it right.

Sarah had been the complete opposite to Hannah. Overly concerned about her being back at work when her father's funeral was only yesterday. She was just like Jack! Neither of them understood that she was alright. Except for the numb feeling she still had inside, and how everything seemed to be a shade too bright. Standing out in technicolour when it was at its worst. She could hear everything from a distance, as if it was crystal clear, and that was strange too. She also seemed to know exactly what was going through people's minds. Although it would have been easy to guess Mark's thoughts, however she was feeling, she couldn't help thinking.

The only thing she was finding it difficult to cope with was them watching her, and he hadn't stopped leering which really was a pain. She was surprised that nothing had been done about him. Given that there were laws to stop sexual harassment. Although she hadn't been subjected to it in the admin jobs she did, and certainly not at the florist shop where she was mostly on her own, he must at least be a borderline case for a disciplinary. Whether or not Mark knew what he was doing, she was surprised that neither Sarah nor Mr Jones had taken the time to have a quiet word with him. Even if it hadn't gone any further than that. Not reaching the company's small, human resources' team. Whilst Hannah either didn't object to it or didn't notice any more, as it had been going on for so long. She also seemed more than capable of looking after herself. Given her attitude, and the ways she spoke to Mark.

Apart from the office politics, it had actually turned into an exciting morning, Chloe thought. Still staring at her computer screen without reading the content on it. Mr Jones had asked her to go with him, to view her first property, and she was glad now that she had worn a suit. She couldn't help thinking it would have made Dad proud. Especially since she had only been with the company for a very short time. Her suit did look more professional than a dress, and Sarah seemed to wear a jacket every day.

Chloe had overheard her asking Mr Jones if he thought it was a good idea for her to go with him, after what had happened. Sarah had been whispering at the time, and said she looked very pale. She had clearly had a shock.

Maybe she needed a little more time to adjust, as she had put it, which Chloe found annoying. Fortunately Mr Jones refused, and told Sarah quite rightly that Chloe Burton was being paid to do a job. So she needed to get on, and learn how to do it.

Chloe took a deep breath, to hide her frustration. All of them were being ridiculous in tiptoeing around her like this. She wasn't a child. It wasn't the same as when her mother had died. At twenty-six years of age she was quite capable of carrying on. Dad always said it was best to be thrown in at the deep end when you were learning something new. You had to make a go of it, if it was a choice between sink or swim. Chloe looked down at the papers on her desk. If anyone had been watching her more thoroughly they would have seen her reading the same page for the last ten minutes, and clearly not taking any of it in. Her thoughts were in too much of a turmoil. She must have told all of them innumerable times, including Jack, that they had to stop worrying about her.

Harry had asked her at the funeral on at least three separate occasions if she was alright. Natalie had done it once, and that was only to be expected. As sisters they were always there for each other, but tended to get on with their own lives. Not to interfere. Natalie wouldn't have been able to do anything anyway. Given how badly she had taken Dad's death, she could barely cope with her own feelings. She said that she wasn't going back to work immediately, teaching the lower fifth at the comprehensive school, whom she said gave her a hard time if she let them.

Chloe thought that it felt a bit strange how everyone was treating her. They seemed to be under the impression that they were whispering, but she could hear every word they said. Even if she hadn't been able to, it was easy to know what they were thinking by the looks on their faces. Dad was right! The only way to stop them from doing it would be to make a success of the job, as quickly as possible, and she fully intended to impress Mr Jones this morning. It was a fantastic opportunity to be accompanying him. The small voice inside her thoughts spoke quite clearly to her then. Reminding her that she would need to concentrate on what she was doing. It was almost time to leave for the appointment. She ought to go to the bathroom first to renew her lipstick, and make sure her hair looked nice.

Chloe found the sales particulars for a similar property to the one they were going to visit, and she read through them in record time. Trying to concentrate on the information they would need to obtain, so the right questions to ask the property owners, and any advice she might be able to give to the new clients about their sale and purchase. Sarah had gone through the interview process with her before she was off work yesterday for the funeral, and Chloe was confident that she could do it. If Mr Jones gave her the opportunity. Not only that, she could do it exceptionally well once she had set her mind to it. Positive energy was coursing through her veins now, to such an extent that she felt compelled to stand up and move about. As what she had read became embedded in her thoughts.

Forgetting about how fast her heart was beating, she was eager to make a start. She glanced again at the time on her computer screen, and grabbed her shoulder bag before making her way to the bathroom. Believing that she was being watched again by three pairs of eyes, Chloe swung her hips. Making sure that she walked as confidently, and sexily as she could. With the intention of showing them all that she fully intended to be a success. Whatever life might throw at her. While the small voice inside her thoughts told her to think of herself instead, as already being a success.

Mr Jones however didn't speak when she followed him to the car park at the rear of the office, a few minutes later. He stopped in front of a new Audi, and stood next to the passenger door. "You had better have these," he said, passing a bunch of keys to her. As Chloe looked down at the blue car in dismay. This wasn't what was meant to happen, she thought quickly. She wasn't a confident driver at the best of times, and had never driven a vehicle like this. Especially a new one.

Mr Jones was looking at his watch. Waiting for her to unlock the car, and get in. "Come on, Chloe," he said, impatiently. It really is a dream to drive, and I have another appointment to prepare for straight after this one. I need to make a few notes on the way there. It isn't far," he added, encouragingly. Regretting now that he hadn't listened to Sarah, and asked Mark to go with him instead. He would already have the engine fired up, with the car in gear. Given that a new Audi was a considerably better option than his old Mini Cooper.

Mr Jones had however made an unspoken rule, to not always go along with Sarah's suggestions. She took a lot for granted as his assistant manager, and there could only be one branch manager at Jenkins & Co: Graham Jones. Whether she liked it or not! What he had forgotten was that Chloe's father had recently been killed in a road traffic accident. Sitting behind the wheel of the vehicle he was driving. It also hadn't entered his head that she might not have driven a car since his death.

As far as he was concerned Chloe had told him at the interview she could drive, and she knew she would have to visit the properties on their books. He didn't realise that she assumed she wouldn't be attending the appointments on her own, and was hoping a colleague would do the driving. As an introvert the possibility of being subjected to someone else's road rage, or having an accident, usually filled her with fear and anxiety.

Whereas on this occasion it was perfectly clear that she wouldn't be able to refuse. So she began to talk quickly about how it wasn't a problem; asking which would be the best way to go, and did he think they would be able to persuade the vendors to give Jenkins & Co their property to sell. The words flowed smoothly, and super fast. If she had been asked to repeat them, it was unlikely that she would have been able to. Although she could easily have said something else instead. Chloe felt the surge of energy flowing strongly through her veins. Giving her all the confidence she needed to unlock the car; get in, and put the key in the ignition. Not pausing once, as her breathing rate became faster and faster.

Until Mr Jones reminded her that he had to collect his thoughts, and make a few notes. As he would be delivering a report to one of the company directors on the performance of the branch. Her name would of course be mentioned, as the latest employee to join them, and he hoped to be able to give a glowing report of what she had done so far. It was at that point Chloe knew she couldn't fail to impress him. She drove the car faultlessly out of the car park; indicated, and manoeuvred it onto the main road. Taking the route which Mr Jones had told her to. Without the necessity of asking him to repeat his earlier directions.

The property in Carlton Avenue wasn't far away, and they arrived without mishap in less than fifteen minutes. Chloe didn't notice any of the scenery or picturesque country lanes they were travelling along, which Jack would no doubt have been able to describe enthusiastically. Everything flew by the car windows in a blur, as she concentrated on driving impeccably. Not once grinding the gears as Mark was prone to do. Something which Mr Jones mentioned a couple of times.

Nevertheless Chloe still felt terrified during the entire journey. Not of crashing the new Audi, but failing to make the right impression on her manager. There was so much she could get wrong, she thought to herself over and over again, but it was as if there wasn't any chance of this happening. Even the roads were almost empty, and she did everything correctly.

After they reached their destination, and while Mr Jones was undoing his seat belt, he told her to leave the talking to him. Chloe frowned. That surely wasn't why she had come? How could she impress anyone, if she didn't say anything? She looked at the manager's face, and blushed. It was easy to see that he thought she talked too much! She felt frustrated by this. He really was an infuriating man, and Chloe didn't know if she could keep quiet for the entire visit. Given how much energy inside her was waiting to be released. Irrespective of this, and knowing she shouldn't argue with him. she said meekly that she wouldn't say a word. Despite it not turning out quite like that, once they were inside the semi-detached house.

She was enthusiastic about the fixtures and fittings; said how much she loved the wallpaper, and carpets which the owners had included in the sale price. Unable to leave it at that, she asked them then if they also intended to leave the curtains. Since they matched the carpet in the sitting room beautifully. Persuading Mr and Mrs Morton to agree. Telling Chloe that they hadn't actually intended to but, since she had mentioned it, they would. Despite the looks of annoyance she received from Mr Jones, Chloe seemed unable to stop talking. Even telling them one of Jack's amusing anecdotes at one point, which she thought afterwards appeared to make the manager's blood boil.

In the end she asked him quietly if she could wait in the car, as she was feeling nauseous, and he readily agreed. Not without looking at her first in distaste. Her saving grace had been Mrs Morton's enthusiastic approval of Mr Jones' young assistant, after Chloe had left, and how well he had trained her. It was a pity she was feeling unwell as they had enjoyed the visit very much. Jenkins & Co had instructions from them to sell their house, and help them buy the next one.

Chloe could tell that Mr Jones still wasn't completely satisfied with her behaviour, but delighted by the outcome of the meeting. So despite remarking on her talkativeness, he moved on swiftly to telling her the price they would use to market the property, and amount of commission Jenkins & Co could expect to receive from this.

Meanwhile Hannah and Mark had been left alone in the office, after Sarah had taken an early lunch. Hannah had locked the front door, intending to say the catch had slipped down if anyone asked, and Mark had put his feet on his desk. While she sat down next to him, and was scrolling through her phone. Despite Sarah telling them both quite sternly that she expected them to get on with their work.

"I don't know why Sarah thinks we should do anything when it's almost Christmas, and Chloe Burton is out swanning around with the manager. She has only been here for five minutes. It makes me sick!" Hannah said, trying to get Mark started again on how it should have been him. Hoping too that he would make life difficult for Chloe, if he thought she was taking his place. Mark could be very childish.

Hannah hadn't been able to get over Chloe wearing an expensive suit to work. It had obviously cost a lot of money, and she was so skinny. It really wasn't fair. At least she wasn't wearing the killer heeled boots today. Hannah didn't think she would have been able to speak to her ever again, or be remotely polite if she had done. Her own boots, which she had loved before seeing Chloe's, were rubbing her feet and had become a constant reminder of how awful they looked. Cheap, and nasty! It didn't matter how hard she tried, something always seemed to come along to knock her back. Women like Chloe had it all. Even stupid Mr Jones obviously fancied the pants off her.

Hannah looked at Mark, and frowned. Maybe she had been too hasty in turning him down. He must earn a lot more than she did; was unattached as far as she knew, and she could change him. She decided to start being nice to him. Just to see what happened. "Mark, honey, do you want me to go and get you a sandwich," she said, smiling invitingly. "I can be back before Sarah. She's gone to meet her friend in the cafe, and she is always gone for an hour when that happens."

Mark looked at her in surprise. Wondering what she was up to now. Whatever it might be, he wasn't about to fall for it. "No, thanks. I'm alright. I've brought a protein shake. I need to build more muscle," he muttered. Taking his feet off the desk, to sit up straight in his chair and push his shoulders back. It was something else he had been practising in the mirror recently, and had been intending to keep for Chloe's benefit. There was however no harm in practising it on Hannah in the meantime.

Jamie, his best mate, had been talking about body language last night. He was about to qualify as an accountant, and earn a load of cash. So in Mark's opinion, was someone worth listening to. A group of them had gone to the pub. He glanced at Hannah who was looking at her phone again, and couldn't believe what a lucky escape he had in getting away from her. She definitely wouldn't have fit in with his social group. Especially now that Chloe had come along. He grinned contentedly. It was going to be a great Christmas. He had already taken the plastic mistletoe out of his sock drawer. No self-respecting bachelor like himself ought to be without it. Although he had been tempted by Hannah's offer of a sandwich, he grabbed the plastic shaker with the protein powder inside, and made his way to the kitchen to add some water to it.

She watched him, feeling even worse than she had done earlier. Mum had been difficult this morning about Ryan, her sixteen year old brother, not coming home last night. Even though he was probably at Darren's. Hannah frowned. Chloe didn't know she was born. It was unlikely that her Mum had multiple sclerosis or had been in a wheelchair for the last three years. Money was tight at home with Mum on benefits, and Ryan about to go off the rails. She had found what looked like several ecstasy pills under his wardrobe. Where he had always hidden his secret stuff when he was a kid. Justifying the snooping with the thought that someone had to. Didn't they? Now Mark wasn't even interested in her, and she had never felt so alone in all her life.

It was true that she had started to feel anxious lately. Especially after Chloe had come along, and highlighted all of the things she didn't have. Hannah got up, and made her way quickly to the toilet so that she could cry in peace. Even if she had remembered Chloe recently lost her father, she wouldn't have been overly sympathetic. Her Dad had run off when she was a baby, according to her Mum. In her opinion, Chloe Burton was one of those women who had it all.

CHAPTER 6

Chloe Uses Her Superpower

It had been a long and successful day Chloe thought, as she walked along the pavement after work. Avoiding any of the more obvious patches of ice, and places where she might slip. Glancing from time to time at the Christmas decorations, which sparkled in the shop windows, and hoping Jack wouldn't spoil her good mood when she got home.

She looked up then at the faery lights, and giant snowflakes festooned from the buildings. Stretching from one side of the pavement to the other above her head. Mappingham really did look stunning tonight. She didn't know why, but the lights seemed to be so much brighter this year. It was odd, but as if she was walking through a movie set. Chloe smiled, to herself. Much to her surprise she felt like dancing. Although that probably wasn't the best idea on an icy pavement in the middle of winter!

It had turned into a fantastic day. Even the unexpected visit to Carlton Avenue with Mr Jones, which could quite easily have been a disaster. It was a huge boost to her confidence when he had asked her to go with him. Making her feel as if she could do anything now, and Chloe frowned. All that could easily change, if Jack started going on about her father again. How he thought she ought to be feeling after Dad's funeral. When he couldn't possibly know how she felt, and her heart softened. He was looking after her in the only way he knew how to. She loved him dearly. They would get through this… Together.

She had been thinking about Jack a lot, and had come to the conclusion he must have always had it in him to be overly protective. Even though she hadn't realised it. She also had a sneaking suspicion that jealousy was partially responsible for his behaviour. He clearly wanted to be a famous artist. Since this was likely to take a long time, was it beyond the bounds of possibility that he might be the teeniest bit jealous of her current success? Probably not, but that didn't help either of them. She had made a promise to her Dad, and had to carry on supporting them both from the money she earned. That was just the way it was. Jack really was being shortsighted in trying to stop her.

His interference had also made her feel more anxious. As if she couldn't do any of it, and Chloe felt as if she was treading on eggshells now when they were together. Why couldn't he just leave her to get on with what they had agreed she should do? Even though for him that would be like trying to push the wind. Jack could be incredibly stubborn, and these same thoughts were chasing each other all of the time. She couldn't get any peace from them.

Apart from all that, she had no intention whatsoever of telling him about Mark. He definitely wouldn't be pleased if he knew that Mark had invited her to meet him at the gym tomorrow morning before work. Putting his arm along the back of her chair. Leaving her in no doubt whatsoever that he was coming on to her. Thankfully she had stopped feeling quite so anxious about him, and afraid of what he might do next, the longer she had been in the office. In the end she had dealt with the situation quite easily. Smiling confidently at him when she said thank you, and promised to mention his invitation to Jack. As if it had been extended to both of them when it clearly hadn't.

Mark's arm had slithered from the chair back at top speed, and she was rewarded with what sounded like a grunt before he went back to his own desk. Ignoring her for the rest of the day, and focusing again on Hannah, as if she was the most amazing woman in the world. Even she had seemed surprised by the change of direction he appeared to have taken.

Mr Jones popped into Chloe's thoughts then. Although she didn't find him too disagreeable, she was surprised that he hadn't been given early retirement by now. He was a bit peculiar, with his clammy hands and greasy hair. He certainly didn't fit the slick image portrayed online, by the other staff in the branch offices. She smiled to herself. Mark was more their cup of tea, she thought, and Sarah also looked like an estate agent. Whereas Jonesy, as Jack had taken to calling him, didn't even seem to know how to use the computer software properly. He relied on Sarah to show him how to do what he needed to.

She really was the centre of the office, and a great teacher. Under her guidance, the computer system had been easy enough to operate. She had taught Chloe how to meet and greet clients properly; take instructions from them, and complete the paperwork online. Also answer their more frequently asked questions. Even the accounts system she had been dreading didn't seem too bad after all. Or the complaints procedure, which would need to be followed in the unlikely event that someone wasn't happy with the service she provided, but that definitely wasn't going to happen!

Chloe replayed part of the conversation they had during the afternoon, when Sarah had told her that she was getting on well. The assistant manager had pursed her lips, and Chloe had asked whether she was thinking about Mark. Sarah stared at her, unsure at first whether to reply, then laughed. Telling Chloe that she must be a mind reader. That she shouldn't really be discussing other members of the team with her, but he could be a handful at the best of times. At least when he was with Hannah he wasn't bothering anyone else, and Chloe had laughed too. Sarah said that it was a pity he was always far too eager to make a sale. It made him seem pushy. Whilst some clients needed a little time to make up their own minds. He was his own worst enemy in that respect she had added, before quickly ending the conversation to answer her phone.

Chloe realised with a start that she had been miles away; lost in her thoughts, and was almost home. Her attention turned again to Jack. She had come to the conclusion that the best way to stop him from worrying about her so much would be to distract him. To get him talking about his two other loves: Painting, and Italian food. A smile was fixed on her lips when she opened the front door, and walked into the apartment. The first question was already being asked, as she took off her socks and boots, to pad bare foot into the living room. "Hello, have you had a good day? How is the painting going?" It was an excellent attempt at starting the evening on a positive note.

Jack didn't however have any intention of being distracted from what he wanted to talk about. He had also had all day to think about everything. Although he answered Chloe's question saying that it was fine, then stood up to hug her and ask how her day had been, concern was still clearly etched in his eyes. "I have been thinking about you," he added, kissing her gently. "I didn't text because I didn't know what you would be doing." The words fell into silence, almost as an accusation.

Chloe immediately felt suffocated. This wasn't what she needed from him. Why couldn't he see that? Instead of treating her as if she was an invalid. She knew it wasn't going to be long before he launched into a dissection of what had happened that morning at the doctor's surgery, and she was right.

Jack had absolutely no intention of being sidetracked. He didn't wait for Chloe to say anything else before he carried on speaking. Having come to the conclusion that he would need to assert himself, to get anywhere with the new super-confident Chloe. He had also had a chat with Harry, to see what he thought. Following his brother-in-law's advice, Jack sat on the settee, and patted the cushion next to him. Inviting Chloe to sit down, which she did. Keeping her features carefully under control so that he wouldn't be able to tell how dismayed she felt.

"Now that we have time to talk about it properly, what exactly happened when you saw the Doctor?" He asked, trying to make it sound as if it was the most natural question in the world.

As anticipated, Chloe gave a non-committal reply which didn't tell him any more than he already knew. Essentially that there was nothing wrong with her medically, and her name had been added to the waiting list for counselling in case she needed it. Although that was highly unlikely.

"What I don't understand is why nothing more was done," Jack said, carefully choosing his words. "I know you better than anyone, Chloe, and you really don't seem like yourself."

This was worse than Chloe had imagined it would be. Jack might as well have insisted that she tell him word for word what Doctor Symes and her had talked about. She felt the blood surging through her veins before she erupted. "Jack, will you please stop doing this?" She shouted at him. "You wouldn't be asking me, if you trusted me. It's as if you think I am lying, and you did say that you didn't want to go into the surgery with me. Asking me all of these questions now is unacceptable. I am not a child!" As she finished speaking a couple of angry tears slid down her cheeks.

Jack took these to be a good sign, that she was upset after all, and had simply been hiding it too well when she didn't need to. He could understand it now. Chloe was finally on the verge of crying because her father had died, and the last thing in the world he wanted to do was to upset her any further. "Hey, it's okay," he said, holding his hands up in surrender. "I'm sorry. I have been worried about you, that's all. How was the rest of your day?"

Chloe, in her excitement at the enormous progress she believed she had made at work and now in persuading Jack to back off, immediately launched into what had happened when she went out with Mr Jones. Only to realise very quickly the trap she had fallen into. Instead of Jack being proud of her, as she had wanted him to be, he seemed shocked. Especially after she slipped it into the conversation that she had driven the manager's new car.

"But Jonesy should have driven. Why did he make you do it? That's awful. What if you had an accident? Chloe, you haven't driven a car for a long time," Jack said the words quickly. Unable to keep quiet any longer.

"Please don't start again, Jack! I've had enough. You can't carry on like this every night when I get home from work. It's as if you don't think I'm capable of doing my job," she said, beginning to cry in earnest.

Jack looked shamefaced, and tried to hold her hand. While Chloe snatched it away from him. "I'm sorry. I thought you didn't feel confident driving, that's all. When we had a car I always drove, because you didn't like doing it. Although I never understood why," he added, hoping that this would go some way to appeasing her. "You are a good driver. Just a bit nervous sometimes on the road. The same as you could be frightened as a passenger. While you are telling me now that you have driven someone else's car. Talking about it as if it was nothing. Something I have been trying to get you to do for a long time, without success. I really don't understand you, Chloe!"

A hint of jealousy had crept into Jack's voice, and because he didn't know the real reason for her earlier reticence about driving. He ran his fingers through his hair in exasperation. Suspecting that there was something she had kept from him, but not having a clue what it might be. Making him feel that what was happening had become a bit too weird. "You didn't even have your driving shoes on. Couldn't Mark have done it?" He muttered, unable to keep his frustration under control any longer, before finally exploding. "All of this is too soon after your Dad's accident, for my liking! What is happening to us, and you, Chloe?"

"Jack, it's my job. I had to manage. Didn't I?" Chloe snapped, as she wiped her cheeks with the back of her hand, to remove the tears. Smearing what was left of her makeup. "I couldn't refuse. Mr Jones made it perfectly clear that wasn't an option. He's not a particularly sensitive man. He doesn't seem in the least bit interested in anyone else's problems, and of course I get nervous about making mistakes. That's only natural. He treats me reasonably well, and I don't want to change that by arguing when he has told me to do something. Can't you see how much I want to get on in this job? While all you are doing is trying to stop me, which is ridiculous."

She stared pointedly at him. Daring him to say anything else, which he didn't have any intention of doing. He was only too glad that she finally seemed to be coming out of herself, and talking to him properly. Albeit in a loud voice. "Sarah did try to say she thought I shouldn't go, but he wouldn't listen. As it turned out, everything was okay,"

Chloe said, failing to mention the panic she had felt when getting into the car. Or how hard her heart was beating while everything had seemed surreal. The surge of energy she experienced had allowed her to get beyond it, and achieve what would previously have seemed impossible.

Jack felt torn. He knew Chloe too well, and it was easy to see that there was something wrong. He desperately wanted everything to be the way it had been between them once upon a time. Not make matters worse. He decided to try again, before giving up. At least for tonight. "Chloe, I know this is difficult, but please stop shutting me out. It isn't healthy to bottle everything up inside," Jack said, quietly. Hoping that this time she would open up fully, and they could move on from whatever it was.

"I refuse to lie, Jack, and I can't tell you anything when there is nothing wrong," Chloe said, matter-of-factly. However, noticing the look of disappointment in his eyes, she knew she would have to do better than that to finally distract him. When all she wanted by now was to sit quietly, staring at a movie on Netflix, without really watching it. As her thoughts about work raced through her mind, and how she could possibly do even better tomorrow. She didn't want to wait until Jack was asleep, and she was lying next to him with her eyes wide open. There was little point in closing them, because she slept very little now. Only when she was completely exhausted, but it didn't matter. She was doing it! Keeping her promise to Dad, and Jack. He had to leave her alone, to get on with it. As far as she was concerned, and after today, Chloe Burton was on track to becoming the best estate agent in the British Isles.

"It was the night my father died," she said, eventually. Pulling the woollen throw closer around herself, that was kept on the settee for them to snuggle together underneath.

Watching her shrink into it, Jack couldn't bear it any longer. He pulled her into his arms, and held her against his chest. It was what she used to ask him to do when she was afraid of something. Usually, on the television. Nothing more was said when Chloe turned her face towards him, and began kissing him slowly. Making Jack feel aroused. From the triumphant look in her eyes, it was clear that this had been her intention. Not simply seeking comfort from their proximity to each other.

It was as if she was taunting him now to take control of what she had started, but as soon as he tried to her lips crushed his beneath her own. While her free hand reached down to undo his belt. Letting him know exactly what she wanted him to do next. His final thought was that the old Chloe wouldn't have done that, and had never tried as desperately as she was doing now to undo the top button on his jeans. Jack groaned. Whatever he had intended to do earlier to sort things out was forgotten, and the moment gone.

CHAPTER 7

An Anxious Weekend

It was Saturday morning, with only another week until Christmas. The street market in Mappingham was bustling with activity. Local people were doing their shopping, alongside visitors to the town, and the majority of the stalls had customers crowded around them.

Chloe was pleased they had come. She could tell that Jack was starting to relax. Listening to the laughter around them, and seeing the smiles on children's faces. He had stopped asking her how she was feeling and trying to get her to talk about her father, at least for the time being. Hopefully, this would be a good opportunity to make things better between them. She was trying her best to look cheerful. Not to do anything which Jack could find fault with. To upset their uneasy truce.

She glanced across the pavement at him. Wondering how she could love someone so much, yet feel wary of him. No! Not again. Her heartbeat had quickened. It was a horrible feeling. Chloe frowned, as she looked down at the partially melted snow on the pavement, and kept going. Her thoughts were in turmoil, but carrying on was the only thing she could do. Monday would be here soon, and she could go back to work. Even though no one else seemed to understand, the job was her lifeline. Whatever Jack or anyone else had to say about it, she couldn't let it go. She felt most alive when she was at Jenkins & Co. Doing what she had promised Dad she would. How could any of them want to stop her?

Jack meanwhile might have appeared to be calm and relaxed, but his thoughts were also in turmoil. He didn't have a clue what else to do, to help Chloe. On the one hand, she was the wife a lot of men could only dream of. Especially when he reminded himself of what had happened last night. They didn't even make it into the bedroom, but she also had a dark place inside her he couldn't reach. However much he wanted to, and as hard as he tried. He had started thinking of it as the invisible barrier she wouldn't let him cross. Causing this unnecessary rift between them. He could tell that she still loved him. Thankfully, that wasn't the problem, but the way she was shutting him out didn't stop him from feeling hurt. The new job was obviously at the root of it, and naturally Steve's death. Jack shook his head, as he walked on through the crowd, and started to do what he usually did when life became too intense. He concentrated on thinking about art, and his painting.

Nevertheless it wasn't long before his thoughts turned back to Chloe. Reasoning with himself that the sooner he had an exhibition, and made a few big sales, the quicker she would be able to stop work. Hopefully letting the old version of her shine through again. She had changed too much in too short a time, and things were only getting worse. He hoped that there wasn't anything else she hadn't told him. You could deal with the things you knew about, but the unknown was a different matter.

Chloe was secretive now from time to time. There was something which he couldn't quite put his finger on, and it had started to worry him. Jack groaned inwardly. He would never be able to enjoy the weekend, if he couldn't get his head straight. So he began thinking again about what had happened last night. Focusing on the good bit, as he had called it. Making him smile. That was how he had imagined married life would be.

Jack's attention was soon drawn to the vegetables piled high on the nearest stall, and without saying anything, he made a beeline for them. Chloe meanwhile carried on walking. Thinking that he was still nearby. As he had been since they left the apartment. She looked around anxiously, as soon she realised he had gone. The colour drained from her face. She couldn't lose Jack too! Looking quickly around again, then behind her, she retraced her steps and finally spotted him handing over a five pound note. Before taking a white plastic bag filled with vegetables, from a stallholder. Breathing a sigh of relief, she pushed her way through the crowd, and stood next to him as he waited for his change.

"There you are!" Jack said, sounding pleased to see her when he half-turned from the stall, to shove the coins into the pocket of his jeans. He kissed her cold cheek. "Hey! What's wrong?" He asked, automatically, when he noticed how pale she was.

"Nothing! I just got a bit worried. I couldn't see you," she said, without any expression in her voice.

"Don't be silly, Chloe. I was only getting some vegetables," he replied, without thinking. Stopping himself just in time from making a joke of it, and saying that she could hardly get lost. Since they were only a few minutes walk from the apartment. "I won't leave you," he added, gently when he realised what might have been going through her mind. Taking her arm to walk with her, until they were standing behind the stalls on the pavement. It seemed to be as good a place as any for him to give her a hug. Enclosing her safely, and completely in his arms.

Jack was shocked that it took a few minutes before her breathing became slower. She nodded, after he asked if she felt better. He grinned then, unable to contain his relief. Also certain that he had thought of the perfect solution, to take her mind off what had happened. He suggested that they go and get a Christmas tree. He knew how much she loved decorating the tree, and looking at the faery lights. However, the idea didn't go as well as he had hoped. Chloe's face fell, as soon as he mentioned it, and she wouldn't tell him why. Insisting that there was nothing wrong.

Not knowing what else to do Jack led the way back to the corner of the street, where a local farmer still had several Christmas trees for sale. Chloe would in the past have taken an active part in choosing which one they ought to buy, before he talked to the farmer. Both of them trying to guess which tree might lose the least amount of needles to vacuum up, also be the best height for the room. On this occasion however, Chloe waited in silence. Leaving Jack to make the decision for them. She began then to talk about the tree he had chosen in the loud, and brittle, voice she often used now.

Passersby began looking curiously at her, and Jack's heart sank. He wasn't surprised. It was odd. Even though he knew it was the last thing he should be thinking of, he couldn't help hoping that she wouldn't spoil Christmas. It was one of the things he had been holding onto. Hoping that it might bring a bit of normality back into their lives. Even though it wouldn't be the same without Steve, and he missed him too. However if today was a sign of what was to come, it didn't look as if it would be great.

Chloe had meanwhile launched into a loud monologue about how she would have liked to put some of the Wilson family's decorations on the tree, but it was impossible. Harry hadn't sorted anything out about Dad's belongings. At least so far as she knew, and she looked accusingly at Jack at this point. As if he knew more about it than he should have done. Without pausing for breath, she went on to say that despite Harry being her brother and having gone back to the naval base, he was the only one who had a key. So it wasn't as if she could go and collect the decorations from Dad's apartment. If anyone had thought to give her a key she would have been able to sort everything out by now!

Jack felt embarrassed. The people around them had heard every word Chloe said, and they were being stared at. As a result he began struggling to walk along the pavement. With the large Christmas tree he had bought under his arm, and carrying the plastic bag full of vegetables with his free hand, to which Chloe seemed totally oblivious.

Continuing her monologue as she walked alongside him. Even though he was finding it difficult to negotiate his way through the crowd, without bumping into anyone.

If Jack had been able to, he would have put his arms around her again. He could tell how much she was hurting, but the best he could manage was to make a few non-committal remarks about how they could use the decorations she already had. He told her that he really liked them. They could also buy a few more, if she wanted to. It wasn't going to break the bank, and would be nice to start their own collection. Maybe buying one or two new ones every year, to add to it.

Whilst his real intention was to get her back to the apartment, as quickly as possible, without further mishap. Chloe, who was walking in front of him, didn't reply. She seemed to be miles away again. No doubt thinking about work, Jack thought, irritably. Wondering why he had bothered, trying to make everything right between them. The situation became even worse after they arrived home, and she stood staring at the tree. He had intended to save it until Christmas Day, but decided to give her the Father Christmas ornament he had found in Mappingham's art gallery. In his opinion it was quirky, and fun. It had made him smile, but Chloe barely glanced at it. She didn't seem overly pleased that he had given it to her, and Jack groaned loudly. "What's wrong now?" He said, miserably. Coming to the conclusion that he couldn't do anything to make her happy.

"Nothing! Nothing at all," she replied, with a beaming smile. Glancing down at the Christmas ornament which she appeared to have forgotten was dangling from the piece of string between her fingers. "It's very nice, Jack. Really. Thank you. I love it." Even though she smiled, the warmth didn't reach her eyes, and the tone in her voice was unconvincing.

"Are you sure?" He couldn't help asking, because he needed reassurance. Still desperately wanting to please her, but instead lighting the flames which had been waiting to explode into a raging fire.

"If you must know," she said, with her voice rising. "I can't bear it. How you are treating me, and now you think it's okay to give me something like this. Don't you realise that Father Christmas reminds me of my Dad? He was the one who was always there on Christmas morning. Waiting for me to open my presents under the tree. You can't replace him with a silly ornament like this!"

Jack felt as if his world had been torn apart. How could Chloe be doing this to him? It was hurtful, and surreal. Whatever he did he would never be able to take Steve's place in her heart. He had known that all along, but she couldn't shut him out. He was her husband. They were married! A wave of misery engulfed him, but he couldn't react. It was exactly as he had thought. Chloe wasn't well, that much was obvious now. It was too soon after Steve's death, and she still hadn't shown any real signs of starting to grieve. Unless this was the beginning of it. The other problem was that he really didn't know how to help her.

Trying to stay calm he took the shiny Father Christmas from her hand, and left it on the table. Before going into the kitchen, to put the kettle on. Intending to make some coffee, to diffuse the situation. When he felt her arms creep around his waist, and the warmth of her head and body against his back.

"I'm sorry, Jack. I don't know what came over me," Chloe whispered, kissing his back softly. "I feel so cold inside, I'm really scared." She said the last words in the tiniest of voices.

Jack turned around straightaway, and held her tightly. "We need help, Chloe. I don't know what to do," he said, helplessly before hesitating. Not wanting her to over react to what he was going to say next. "I told you that I would always look after you, and I said it again when we got married. I meant it, Chloe. Please let me ask Dr Symes to arrange an appointment with a counsellor. Someone who will know what to do, and say to you, because I honestly don't any more."

Chloe hid her face against his chest, to give herself time to think about what Jack had said. Maybe the appointments wouldn't interfere with work, and no one had to find out that she was having counselling. She was also starting to be afraid of how quickly her heart was beating, as if it was out of control. Jack would leave her alone too, if she agreed. So that she could focus on her job. Instead of having to pretend any longer that she... Oh, what harm could it do? She probably wouldn't get an appointment for weeks. Her name had only recently been added to the waiting list.

Much to Jack's surprise as he was preparing himself for another argument the longer he waited, Chloe said, "yes! Alright I'll go. I'll see a counsellor, but on one condition.

That you get me an appointment after work or first thing in the morning. So that I can go before the office opens."

At first Jack was unable to believe she had agreed. Thinking that he must have misheard. Until Chloe repeated what she had said. "It'll be for the best, you'll see," he replied, clearly overjoyed. "I know you are worried about your job, Chloe, but there isn't any stigma attached to counselling. Not now. A lot of people have it, and I want us to get back to the way we used to be. For you to feel better."

That was it in a nutshell, Chloe thought, bitterly. Unable to think clearly any longer. The only thought she had was that her agreement to go for counselling wasn't anything to do with the promise she had made to her father. Or letting her do the job in which she had started to excel. As far as she was concerned, Jack wanted everything his own way. Why did he insist that she needed counselling? When she was doing so well at work. She had tried her best to make him happy physically, so that she could do what Dad had wanted for her, but none of it had been enough.

Chloe looked into his eyes, and decided that she couldn't bear the thought of wasting any more of her energy on another argument. Instead of saving it for Monday. "You are right," she said, in the brightest of voices. Smiling at him. "I would love a coffee. Shall we have a takeaway later?" Accepting that there would be little point in her offering to cook for him. She felt tired, but would have had the energy to do it. Chloe was confident of that, but Jack never wanted her to cook because of his own passion for it.

He decided to go along with her suggestion of getting a takeaway, if it made her happy, and both of them liked the local Indian restaurant. So he ordered the food from there. It arrived later, after they had decorated the tree. He ended up finishing her rice, and a good half of the chicken korma she had ordered. Despite trying to persuade her gently, to eat it.

While they were decorating the Christmas tree with the ornaments they had, Chloe had suggested in a bright and breezy voice that they go for a long walk on Sunday. As the weather wasn't supposed to be too bad. Jack agreed, but if they had been able to be honest with each other, they would have discovered that they both felt a sense of dread. At the possibility of them arguing again. When this seemed virtually impossible to avoid. Jack was however trying his best to stay positive, because of Chloe's agreement to see a counsellor. Believing that it could truly be the light at the end of the tunnel.

As they ate he told her more about his painting. How he would like to paint the scenery around the castle, and the ruined stones in the centre. He became quite excited about it. Also that if the weather held he might be able to do a few quick sketches. Promising her it wouldn't take long, as it would be too cold to stand about outside. He had squeezed her hand then, and asked if she would like a glass of wine in the bar across the road. Like they used to do in London. They held hands as they walked there.

Chloe felt it would be alright to talk about work when Jack had almost drunk his first pint of real ale. The words fell from her lips faster, and faster. Repeating much of what she had already told him. Starting with how well she thought everything was going. Even her relationship with Mr Jones was good. She didn't mention Hannah because she wasn't part of her success, or Mark's invitation to go to the gym. She also still didn't say anything about her father, which surprised Jack the most. In particular because she had opened up enough earlier, to say that the Father Christmas he gave her reminded her of him.

When he was on his third pint he felt sufficiently relaxed to be able to mention that she seemed anxious, and he was pleased she had agreed to go for counselling. Chloe stared coldly at him. Wishing she could tell him the truth. That she was only going, because she felt she didn't have any choice. It was exactly the same as the appointment with Doctor Symes, and Jack trying to get her to eat more. The pressure he was putting on her was making her feel anxious. Mostly that he would try to stop her from going to work. Not believing that she would be able to cope, because she wasn't well enough. When that wasn't the case at all.

Sensing the silence could be developing into something more serious again, Jack decided to change the subject quickly. Asking Chloe if she would like to WhatsApp Natalie tomorrow. Before making the mistake of adding that Harry had told him the Doctor had given her some tablets to help her cope. Instead of letting Chloe find this out for herself from the conversation with her sister.

Chloe had said sarcastically then, that she was surprised they hadn't also organised counselling for Natalie! After that the silence between them became as solid as a brick wall, and when Chloe refused to have another glass of wine, Jack bought himself a pint which he drank quickly before they walked home. Side by side this time, in silence, and without holding hands.

Chloe became talkative again on Sunday, as soon as she opened her eyes. As if the awkwardness between them had never happened, and she even seemed to take an interest while Jack explained the finer points of painting the individual stones of the castle ruins. It had taken him longer to recover from them almost arguing again in the bar, and although he had fallen asleep with his back to her, her limbs had been entwined with his when he woke up. Leading to fast and perfunctory sex, before he got up to make some freshly ground coffee and ciabatta toast, which they had in bed.

Chloe telephoned Natalie on Sunday evening, as he had suggested, and she seemed to try during the day to make amends. Again from talking to Harry, and so far as Jack knew, Natalie and her hadn't spoken since the funeral. When she did call her sister he didn't know what they talked about, because Chloe took her mobile phone into the bedroom. Jack had thought they were close, but Harry refuted this. Telling him that it was an ongoing competition between his sisters when they were growing up, as to who got the most of their father's attention. While Jack was getting the distinct impression that Chloe was becoming jealous now of his relationship with Harry. So he didn't mention anything else they had discussed.

He didn't believe that Chloe would go back on her agreement to see a counsellor, and he intended to ring the surgery as early as possible on Monday morning to make the arrangements. Feeling pleased for once, that she insisted on going to work early.

CHAPTER 8

Her First Counselling Session

Jack was delighted when he managed to arrange a counselling session for Chloe during the first week in January, and that she didn't try to stop him from going with her. The appointment was at eight o'clock in the morning, and it would take them at least thirty minutes to walk there. Chloe insisted that this was what she wanted to do. Instead of taking the bus which stopped almost outside their apartment, and would have dropped them off opposite the health centre on the edge of Mappingham.

She became irritable when Jack tried to get her to change her mind. Before finally admitting that she was worried the bus wouldn't come or arrive too late for the appointment. He took this as a good sign, and assumed that she now wanted to go. Whereas she simply wanted to get it over, and done with. Jack didn't mention it again. Since he had also made the mistake of trying to get her to eat some breakfast, which led to another disagreement. After she had refused to eat even a small bowl of cereal. Telling him quite firmly that she wasn't hungry, and he ought to stop pestering her about food.

Nevertheless she did try to coach him at one point about what to say in the meeting, and it seemed clear to

Jack from the tone in her voice that she expected him to be on his best behaviour. Making him feel as if he was going to school for the first time with his Mum. He started to wonder if this was how she behaved at work, and he hoped not. The thought of what she might actually be like at Jenkins & Co sent him into an even worse mood. Until he felt completely fed up, then confused. When her mood changed again, and became more upbeat.

He stared at Chloe in disbelief. The way she was behaving now was as if she felt she could conquer the world. Deciding not to say anything else apart from reminding her that she needed to tell the counsellor, Colin Maitland, the truth. Not gloss over anything, or hide how she was feeling. Much to Jack's surprise, she didn't argue this time. Only looked at him scornfully, before reminding him that she wasn't stupid. Something else which the old Chloe wouldn't have done, he thought. She would have been seeking reassurance by now, that everything was going to be okay, and asking him to do most of the talking when they got there. As he was the extrovert side of their relationship, so used to doing that, and as an introvert she wasn't.

Given the change in her behaviour Jack wasn't however in the least surprised when Chloe led the way into the meeting room at the health centre, and immediately took charge of the introductions in a loud voice. Much to his embarrassment she looked at her watch before they sat down, and said quite firmly that she didn't want to be late for work. Jack was relieved that Colin Maitland, who was in his early fifties, seemed completely at ease with what was happening. As if he had seen it all before. He didn't appear to take offence at Chloe's abrupt behaviour, which in Jack's opinion bordered on rudeness. Especially when Colin had made an effort to see them before his appointments began at nine o'clock.

The counsellor cleared his throat, and spoke in a calm and reassuring manner. Realising just how anxious Chloe was, despite her attempt at hiding it under a show of confidence. "Let me explain first of all that this is an introductory session for us to get to know each other; set up a programme to meet Chloe's needs, and consider the available options to help reduce her anxiety levels. Please don't be alarmed by the term: cognitive behavioural therapy. All it means is that Chloe and I will be talking to each other at the meetings. The idea is to find the best way to help you manage your feelings, Chloe, and any problems you might be having in everyday life. I shall try to help you find other ways to think about them, which will hopefully make you feel less anxious. You will have the opportunity to put any changes we agree into practice, and we can discuss how you got on at the next meeting.

I understand you have recently lost your father. My condolences," Colin said, gently. Pausing to assess her reaction. When Chloe's facial expression didn't alter, nor did she reach for a handkerchief as the majority of patients would have done at this point, he carried on talking. "It's natural to be more anxious after the death of a close family member, and there may of course be other things which are contributing to this."

Chloe interrupted him then. Quickly reminding Colin that her father's death occurred not long after she had started a new job, and this was important. Jack's heart sank. Wondering now whether he ought to say something, but Chloe had already started talking about Jenkins & Co. She seemed determined to keep control of the meeting.

As soon as she paused for breath, Colin seized the opportunity to carry on telling her about the sessions she was booked in for, and the information he was obliged to pass on to patients. "Yes, thank you, Chloe. We shall certainly be exploring those areas," he said, clearing his throat again, loudly. "In my experience the success of the therapy will depend on how honest you are about your feelings. With me, and yourself. It usually takes anywhere between six to twenty-four sessions for anxiety to reach a manageable level, depending on how we get on. Given the state of my diary, we should be able to meet once every two weeks. Today is for one hour, and the other meetings will be thirty minutes each."

As Chloe was staring at her hands by this time, having apparently lost interest, Colin turned to Jack and thanked him for coming. He liked the look of the young man sitting in front of him, who was clearly trying his best to support his wife. It wasn't long however before Chloe began to talk again about her job, and the conversation began in earnest between Colin and her. Although she did most of the talking.

As Jack listened he couldn't help noticing that she only provided the minimum of information. Followed by short, and succinct replies to Colin's questions. So that he was given only the bare bones of their lives. Without any reference to her feelings, which in Jack's opinion were what actually mattered.

Colin had also come to the same conclusion, and found it interesting that she was trying to shut him out. Clearly Chloe Burton was afraid of something, and of letting him get too close to find out what that was. He decided that it was time to change direction. Since he was also conscious of the clock ticking. Maybe it would be the best option to get Jack talking, in case he didn't come to any more of the appointments. It might reveal whether there were any problems in their relationship, and again, what could be at the root of her anxiety. Even at this early stage it seemed unlikely to be only as a result of grief.

"How did you celebrate Christmas?" Colin said, smiling at both of them. Knowing that this could often be difficult, at the best of times.

Chloe launched into a superficial account of what had happened. "As you can imagine, it wasn't the best of days," she said, matter of factly. " We even ended up arguing." She laughed, uncertainly. "My brother, Harry, was in Portsmouth. He had to get back to work, but my sister came to us. Jack and I don't have a car but Natalie does, so this was the easiest option. Jack likes to cook, and he wanted to make lunch. Since we couldn't…" She hesitated, unable to carry on, but instead of bursting into tears her voice became louder and more authoritative when she spoke again. "As we obviously couldn't go to the restaurant where Dad had booked us in for Christmas lunch."

"And what did you make of the day, Jack?" Colin said, quickly. Chloe was about to respond when, feeling confused, she realised that he had asked Jack the question. She stared at him, as Colin added, "Chloe has already mentioned that the day ended up in you having an argument."

"It wasn't all bad," Jack mumbled, in his defence. "I enjoy cooking, and Chloe and Nat seemed to like the food. It happened afterwards when they were talking, and I went back into the kitchen to sort out the Christmas pudding."

Chloe couldn't remain silent any longer, and she interrupted him. "It was all very silly, Colin. Nothing at all to be concerned about. My sister qualified as a teacher a few years ago. Dad was always very proud of her. Whereas I worked as an administrative assistant, and took a job in a florist's shop in London, after I got my degree. I was happy enough doing that. There wasn't a lot of pressure, and I liked the work. However it was clear that Dad thought she had done much better than I had. I suppose I felt in the end that he was disappointed in me. Harry had also done well in the Navy.

It became Dad's dearest wish that I should train to be an estate agent when we moved to Mappingham, and he found out that Jenkins & Co had a vacancy. He persuaded me to apply for the job. He helped me work on my interview technique, and I was fortunate to get it. The problem now is that both my husband and sister seem determined to make me have some time off work. The manager has said that I am doing very well, and I don't see any need to stay at home. More importantly, I promised my father that

I would do my best to make the job a success. Obviously I can't do that if I don't go to work."

"How do you feel about this, Jack?" Colin asked, turning to him.

When Jack looked uncomfortable, Colin checked with Chloe that she was still happy for her husband to be part of the meeting. After she grudgingly said yes, he turned back to Jack and waited for him to answer.

"Alright if I have to say it, I think you have taken all of this the wrong way, Chloe. Your Dad loved you. Anyone could see that. Nat and I are worried. We both think that you went back to work too soon after he passed, and all you can think about now is your job. You don't seem to be grieving. You haven't even cried, despite how close the two of you were, and before this happened you certainly didn't carry on the way you are doing now. It was completely out of character for you to argue with Natalie like that on Christmas Day." He hesitated. Not wishing to say anything else that might hurt her, but Colin was clearly waiting for him to carry on. "It spoiled the day!" Jack said finally, wishing that the ground would open up and swallow him.

"Trust you to take her side!" Chloe said, erupting angrily. "You don't know what it was like when I was growing up. Especially after Mum died! It was always as if I had a lot more to prove to Dad. Even when he died I still couldn't be the one to be told first. Harry had already spoken to Natalie, then he told you. Asking you to pass the message onto me. Why couldn't I have been told first?"

"Oh, Chloe, that's just how it happened. I was there with you, and Harry had already broken the news to your sister. It may have escaped your notice but I am also now a member of this family!" Jack said, clearly dismayed.

"Did you feel that your father loved Natalie more than you?" Colin said, quite brutally Jack thought. Wishing that he hadn't asked her this.

A tear slid down Chloe's cheek, as she said,"yes." Almost so quietly that neither of them heard it.

Jack reached across the short distance between their chairs and put his hand on her arm. "It wasn't a question of taking sides, Chloe. Colin asked us to answer him honestly, and that's what I did. You know that Natalie went home not long afterwards. It's hard for her too, losing Steve, and she was going home to an empty apartment. At least we have each other. She was so eager to be gone she left without eating her pudding," he finished, lamely.

"You are always thinking about food, Jack. You really are impossible! If we are talking about things that make me anxious, why do you insist on trying to get me to eat more? It's controlling, and I don't like it. Dad used to make sure I was always eating enough when I was a child," she said, "and I grew up without the need for you to do it too." Her words pushed Jack into saying what came next.

"I can't believe you have said that, Chloe. Or think I am trying to control you. When all I am doing is making sure you have a healthy diet. I think the world of you. What is wrong with you? I am only trying to look after you, and all you do is keep pushing me away."

Jack put his head in his hands, feeling completely out of his depth by this time. "I can't carry on like this! You have changed so much, I am starting to wonder if you are the same woman I married. You would never have done anything like that in the past to Natalie, or me. It isn't in your nature to be mean spirited," he said, forgetting his earlier reticence about Colin being in the room with them. Focusing his attention completely, on Chloe and himself.

Meanwhile Colin was delighted that they had opened up to this extent, especially when it was only the first meeting. This was the first step in him being able to help Chloe. Some patients took several sessions before they were comfortable enough to release pent up feelings like this. If he was right, there was a lot going on here under the surface, and he still didn't know all of it. Jack appeared to be straightforward enough. Chloe however was a lot more complex, and this was about her which he didn't intend to lose sight of. He glanced at the clock on the opposite wall, and saw that they had almost reached the end of the session.

Both Chloe and Jack were by now staring down at the carpet. Stony faced, and clearly upset. Probably with themselves, and each other, Colin thought. Whilst Chloe felt anxious at having revealed as much as she had done in her loud and brittle voice. Whereas Jack was fed up that he had lost his temper, which was something he certainly didn't intend to do.

"Thank you, both. I feel as if we have made a lot of progress," Colin said, calmly. "I am afraid that we have run out of time, but I will send you some information online about the meditation techniques I would like you to try, Chloe. We'll talk about them next time, and there'll be a couple of exercise videos to watch. The more exercise you can get the better. Can I also suggest yoga? I don't know if this is something which you already do, or have done. It can be wonderfully relaxing. You might also find it useful to join a class. I'll send details of the one Mandy White runs here at the centre, and please don't worry! We can explore your feelings and the different ways you might have handled the situation with Natalie, at our next meeting," He glanced at Chloe who was still staring at the carpet, then Jack looking back at him.

"You mustn't be too hard on yourselves. Either of you," Colin added, quickly. "You have gone through some major life changes in quick succession. Any of which would have the potential to turn your world upside down. Moving from London was a huge step for anyone to take, and I can tell how hurtful you find your father's loss, Chloe. You have done the right thing in getting everything out into the open. If there is anything else you need to tell me, please let me know next time, and I'll see you again." Colin said, standing up to show that their meeting was over. Shaking hands first with Chloe then Jack. Sensing that this was what she would expect him to do.

"If you would prefer to attend any of the sessions on your own, Chloe, then it is of course your prerogative to do so. The decision is yours," he said quietly to her, after Jack had walked through the door. Even though he hoped that they would both attend next time, he felt under an obligation to remind her of this since she was the one receiving the therapy.

Chloe nodded as she left the room, and neither Jack nor her spoke until they were outside in the fresh air. When she immediately reverted to her bright, and brisk self. "Phew! That's over, and done with now," she said, almost as if she was checking it off a mental to do list. "I don't think we need to bother going again. There isn't anything wrong." She hesitated then, noticing the stern look on Jack's face. "Even if you disagree, it's nothing we can't sort out by ourselves. You heard what Colin said. All he intends to do is talk to me."

Jack shook his head, sadly. "Chloe, I think there'll be a bit more to it than that. Look at how we ended up arguing again, and this was only the first session! Colin will need to know a lot more about what has been happening. To help you stop overreacting, and deal with the loss of your Dad. You might think you can hide it, but not from me. I've seen how ill you look sometimes. Didn't you hear him say that the things we have gone through are life changing, and that you will need to carry on with the sessions?" Jack said, earnestly. Looking into Chloe's eyes and hoping she would agree.

He was worried now about dealing with the aftermath of the meeting when they got home. This was like nothing else he had experienced so far in his life, and even if Chloe wasn't, he was glad of the counsellor's support. Not having anyone else to turn to, only possibly Harry, which in his eyes would mean he had failed as a husband.

Meanwhile Chloe had listened to Jack's voice in the background, as everything else became a blur, and wished he would put his arm around her. Saying that everything would be alright, but she could tell that this wasn't going to happen. She felt frightened. Jack looked shattered, overwhelmed even. He would be going back to the apartment without her. She was going to work. As she had promised Dad and him she would. So that he could carry on painting.

A part of her also wished that she had admitted to Colin, her heart could start racing at any time, and her head often ached. As it was doing now. Everything in the street seemed so loud, but she could have heard a pin drop on the pavement opposite. Some of the things about the office did worry her. Mr Jones could be impatient, and didn't seem interested in anyone else's problems. Least of all hers. Making her feel nervous, and anxious about making mistakes. Mark was simply a nightmare, and Hannah to a lesser extent. There was no way out. Only to do as she had promised. She took a deep breath.

"Jack, what an old grump you are! I am fine. I'll see you tonight," she said, stepping forward to kiss him quickly on the cheek. Before starting to run to catch the bus pulling up nearby. The number fifty-seven would take her to the High Street, and the office. Not doubting for a second that she might be too late to catch it.

Chloe hadn't said that she would carry on seeing Colin, Jack thought bitterly. As he watched the bus depart and she looked straight ahead. Forgetting, or not bothering, to wave from the window. He no longer knew.

CHAPTER 9

A Birthday Party For Chloe

A few days later Chloe was walking along the High Street, holding onto Jack's arm. She was wearing her highest heels, and wished they could go home. She felt awkward doing this. Their relationship had been strained since the counselling session, and spending the evening with a lot of other people was the last thing she wanted to do.

Jack was also lost in thought. After the meeting he had eventually become absorbed in painting a new canvas, and was feeling satisfied with it by the time Chloe came home from work. He had decided not to pressurise her about seeing Colin Maitland, but to let everything settle down again first. He still wasn't sure whether this was his way of avoiding the truth, that their married life wasn't what he had expected. Or because he didn't have the answers to fix what was happening, and he was afraid. If he was being honest with himself, he was also finding it hard being on his own all day. So it would be great to have a break tonight, and meet some new people.

Although very pale, Chloe had seemed confident after work on the day of the meeting. Unable to stop talking about the property she had sold, and how the others had clapped when Sarah told them that she was now officially launched. Jack felt sorry that he hadn't been able to be as enthusiastic about it as she was, and he blamed himself. Chloe was doing her best. Not only for her Dad, but him. Something he knew he had lost sight of, and shouldn't have done. If only she would take a few days off and forget about work, they could spend some quality time together sorting things out. He also wouldn't feel as guilty that she was the one out there, earning the money for them to live on, even though she wasn't well.

His guilty feelings had been worse since their talk with Colin, and seeing how anxious Chloe had become. It was incredible that she had the energy to keep going, as she did. He still hadn't been able to put any of this into words because of the rift between them, but he was determined to try harder, To make tonight a success. Although he wasn't sure whether or not it was a blessing in disguise, that Natalie had turned up unexpectedly.

Chloe wished that she knew what Jack was thinking. He hadn't said another word about the counselling session, as she had expected him to, and the silence was worse. He seemed to be impatient to get to the Green Man public house, to meet everyone from the office who had decided it would be a fantastic opportunity to get to know him. Also she guessed, to find out more about her. When they discovered from Sarah that it was her birthday on the ninth of January.

Jack wasn't walking as slowly as he usually did, Chloe thought with disdain. As she glanced at Natalie, walking along the pavement on the other side of him. Apparently not having any problem in keeping up. She didn't want to share Jack with her! An image flashed through her mind then, of her father dying alone on another cold night like this. Chloe's heart began hammering inside her chest, and the surge of energy which accompanied it made her walk quicker. She no longer needed to ask either of them to slow down.

Meanwhile Natalie had also been thinking about everything that had happened. She decided that it would be a good excuse to turn up on her sister's birthday, as a surprise. They hadn't spoken since Christmas, and she was also feeling guilty. When they had argued it had been the last thing she wanted to do, and Jack was right. Chloe wasn't herself. She overreacted to a lot of what was said to her. It had been obvious that she wasn't getting on very well with him, which was awful. Since they had only just got married.

Before they left the apartment, Natalie asked Chloe about the counselling sessions, and she had given a non-committal reply. Without saying exactly what she thought. She had spoken flippantly about the meditation exercises Colin had sent, and said the last she felt like doing after work was exercising. Natalie could tell that Jack was upset by her response. He had gone into the bedroom, to let them carry on talking by themselves. Chloe whispered to Natalie then that she didn't really want to go to any more of the sessions, and had only attended the first one because Jack wanted her to. She added that she didn't particularly like Colin.

Meanwhile Jack was feeling confused, and trapped. If he spoke for longer than two minutes to Natalie, he could tell that Chloe didn't like it, and she was his sister-in-law! The way she behaved now was ridiculous. It was even worse than he had told Colin. The argument with Natalie went on for most of Christmas day. After he had walked with her back to her car, carrying some leftovers and presents, Chloe didn't speak to him for most of the evening. Only mumbled from time to time, which ended in them both drinking far too much. Even the special bottle of wine they had put aside for New Year.

He couldn't understand Chloe at all. Not now. All he had been doing was helping Natalie, as the gentleman he tried to be, and he did feel sorry for her. She was going home to an empty apartment. There wasn't any reason why she shouldn't have stayed longer with them. Other than that Chloe had behaved unreasonably. Making her sister feel uncomfortable, and ultimately unwanted. Although he couldn't tell her this, the mood she was in.

Despite Christmas Day ending with them having passionate sex, it hadn't made either of them feel any better the following morning. Jack had started to think that lust might be the only thing holding their marriage together, and the novelty of Chloe being the dominant one had begun to wear off. Jack frowned. He was a softie at heart, but why shouldn't he simply like being in love with the woman he thought he had married? Whereas Chloe seemed insatiable now. Some of the suggestions she was starting to make weren't really what he wanted to do. Jack almost smiled then. Her behaviour was making him feel anxious! Also doubtful that the agreement for her to be the bread-winner, albeit temporarily, had been such a great idea.

Jack quickened his step, without realising it. He truly loved the soft, and feminine side of Chloe which was still there. Somewhere underneath all this, and he hoped with every fibre of his being that she wouldn't change any more. The job was at the root of it, he was certain. What else could it be? He was looking forward to this evening for another reason. It would give him an opportunity to meet the competition. Especially since Chloe hadn't been overly keen for him to accept Sarah's invitation, and had tried her best to put him off. Using any number of excuses from how he would hate it, to being bored. Not once thinking that he would actually like to go. Or that he missed going out socially.

When they arrived at the Green Man, Jack held the door open for Chloe and Natalie. Before following them into the warm, and cosy lounge bar. Chloe strode through the door. Making a beeline for the group of people, sitting in the farthest corner, around a table filled with glasses. Mark cheered, and raised his glass. While the customers nearby soon joined Jenkins & Co in singing happy birthday. Much to Chloe's dismay when she felt everyone's eyes on her. All she wanted to do was hide behind Jack, but she could tell from the huge grin on his face that he was loving every minute of it.

Retaking control of the situation, as soon as the noise died down, she introduced everyone to each other. Jack was invited straightaway to sit between Hannah and Mark, who made a space for him on the opposite side of the table to Natalie and Chloe. Mark had also brought his friend, Jamie, the almost qualified accountant. To make the numbers up, he said. He was obviously intrigued by Natalie, and her similarity in appearance to Chloe. Having established that she wasn't wearing a wedding ring, Mark thought that his luck could have changed. He raised himself up on his stool, until he was satisfied he was looking his best. Sarah asked them what they would like to drink, and insisted on going to the bar. Refusing Jack's offer to help.

It wasn't long however before Chloe began to feel jealous of how well Hannah was getting on with Jack. She didn't know that Hannah was only doing it to annoy her, at least at first. Also to pay Mark back for turning her down, which she still hadn't forgotten, but she soon found herself having fun. Enjoying the evening much more than she thought she would. Jack really was cool! Despite being incredibly sexy he was also interesting, and he told her a lot of things she enjoyed hearing. It wasn't often that anything interested her enough to ask questions, but she did. He also listened politely when she gave her opinion. Although it did make him laugh sometimes, and she hoped he wasn't making fun of her. Until she caught his eye, and he winked. She could have forgiven him anything after that.

It looked to everyone else, especially Chloe, as if there was a definite spark between them. One which had been lit. Mark meanwhile was looking extremely dejected that he couldn't catch Natalie's eye, however hard he tried, and all of the attention he would usually get from Hannah was being given to Jack. Sarah too seemed to be quite taken with him, he thought. Even old Jonesy looked impressed when Jack began talking about his visit to Florence, to look at the paintings and sculpture. Followed by how he was working towards having his own exhibition. He didn't seem to find Jamie's views on accountancy practises for estate agents nearly as interesting.

It was enough for Hannah, to know that she had been right all along. Chloe did have a rich husband. Okay, he might not be very rich at the moment, but soon would be. She was glad that she had put on even more mascara than usual. To be able to flutter her eyelashes, and flirt with him. Although Jack noticed her doing it and they were having fun, he felt sorry for leading her on. He was trying to make Chloe notice him again, to realise what she was missing. Even though it was her birthday, making him feel guilty again, it could be the only chance he got to do it for a while.

He didn't like the accountant, one little bit, and Mark was a nerd which meant he was unlikely to get anywhere near Chloe. She wouldn't be particularly interested in him. He could tell. She seemed to be engrossed now in talking to Natalie, and he breathed a sigh of relief. At least something good would come from tonight, if they became friends again.

Chloe was however becoming very anxious about everyone making a fuss of Jack. As usual, he had become the life and soul of the party. Even Mark was joining in the banter, and trying to compete with him in talking about cars which didn't really interest Jack. Except for the Lamborghini he said he would like to own one day, but it was Italian. So bound to influence his decision on which would be the best car to have.

It came to her then, totally out of the blue, how much she wished her father could have been there. He would have loved to see the people she worked with, and how she had already become an integral part of Jenkins & Co. She hoped she looked okay. She wasn't wearing anything new, but the top was from Mango. She had changed her lipstick to a brighter shade of red, which she thought Jack didn't particularly like. Even though he said that he did, he had frowned. She normally wore pale pink, but she was a lot more confident now. So why not?

She glanced at Natalie who had brought her a card and presents, as a peace offering. A new book she had been meaning to read, along with a bright blue scarf which she loved. Natalie had whispered sorry when she came into the apartment, and hugged her. Saying too, that they ought to become closer. Not argue. Dad wouldn't have liked it, to which Chloe had to agree, and things seemed to be a lot better after that.

Jack was meanwhile asking Hannah about her family. She told him that her grandmother had arrived in the United Kingdom when she was a young woman, and hadn't left after she met her grandfather who lived in Mappingham. "I would love to go to Italy. Nonna came from Venice, but I can't afford it. Not at the moment," Hannah said, wistfully.

"You must go! You would love it there, Hannah. The sunshine, and the food; St. Mark's square; the history, and the art. It's stunning. I understand from Chloe that Italian men are apparently to die for," Jack said, with a twinkle in his eye. At least she certainly felt that way about the one who took us on his gondolier."

Hannah listened to him talking, and knew that she wouldn't have taken her eyes off him if he had been her husband. It was typical of Chloe. Not to appreciate what she had.

"I would love to go," she replied. "With you!"

Jack spluttered into his beer, trying to recover from his surprise, but Hannah was already covering her tracks. "Oops, I have had too much wine. Although it would be nice," she grinned, cheekily, and began to laugh.

Jack soon joined in, but decided he had better remind her that Chloe was sitting opposite them. Hannah's response was to ask him if he believed that anything was possible, and he couldn't say no. If you wanted it badly enough. Making them both laugh, even more uproariously this time. Before he winked at her again, as the beer made him feel super friendly, and he asked everyone what they would like to drink. Making his way to the bar with Jamie, who had offered to help him carry the glasses.

Hannah stared smugly at Jack, as he walked away. Having done what she had intended to. He wouldn't forget their conversation in a hurry. When he was feeling low, he might well wonder about anything being possible. It had been easy enough. After she had overheard Chloe talking to Sarah about his passion for Italy, and having her grandmother to thank for the rest.

Hannah's thoughts were interrupted by Mark, who didn't like what he suspected had been happening under his nose. He didn't hold a grudge against Jack, but this was his patch. He already had Chloe, who looked amazing tonight. He had found it difficult to stop himself from staring at her. Also her sister, Natalie, whom he thought wasn't as good looking but still alright. Hannah was however a different matter, They were mates, and had a history. Although she might not be inclined to agree with him about that, she had still given him a kiss when they left the office on Christmas Eve. After he had taken the plastic mistletoe he usually carried at this time of year from his pocket. Holding it above their heads, outside in the snow.

Mark moved, to sit on the stool Jack had recently left, and nudged Hannah none too gently with his elbow. "What are you up to now?" He asked. Not really expecting her to tell him, but Hannah could be full of surprises. The latest being that if she was to remove Jack from the picture, it would leave the way clear for him to move in on Chloe. He looked at her expectantly, with a certain amount of excitement. Hoping she would tell him next that she had a date with Jack. Only to be disappointed when she replied, quite innocently, "I'm only joking, Mark!" Unable to hear her add under her breath, "but you never know what might happen."

Jack meanwhile was finding it difficult to concentrate on remembering what everyone was drinking, and had to be reminded by Jamie. Chloe hadn't talked a lot about Hannah. He had the feeling she didn't think she was very important. Jack didn't however feel the same way. As far as he was concerned Hannah was feisty; a lot of fun, and definitely up for a laugh. A true breath of fresh air.

He still couldn't believe she had asked him if he thought anything was possible. What a chat up line that was! If ever he had heard one, and he had heard a few over the years. She was certainly not in Chloe's league, but she had somehow got under his skin. Even though, for Heaven's sake, he had just got married. He was hardly likely to take her up on it. Was he? She must surely have known that, and it was only harmless banter after all. Although it made him feel good, to wonder what if…

Natalie noticed that Chloe hadn't spoken for a while. She seemed to be preoccupied. Staring at Hannah and Jack talking on the other side of the table. Although it was impossible to hear what they were saying to each other. Natalie pulled her stool closer, so that it would be easier for Chloe and her to talk. "They seem like a nice bunch," she said, smiling as she looked around. Just before Mark stared longingly at her, and she blushed. Averting her eyes quickly. Remembering what Chloe had said about him.

"Everyone seems so confident, and self assured," Chloe said, unexpectedly.

"You are too," Natalie said, feeling surprised, but her sister hadn't finished.

"Even Jack! He is always so quiet, and gentle at home. Not as talkative. Only really interested in his painting."

"And you," Natalie said, quickly. Wondering where this was leading.

"Yes, and me, of course," Chloe said, a little too loudly, with the brittle tone back in her voice. As she looked again at Jack talking to Hannah, and laughing at something she had said.

"They are only having a bit of fun, Chloe. That's all. What's really wrong?" Natalie said, with concern. "Apart from losing Dad, of course." She saw her sister hesitate, before replying.

"It's just that Jack doesn't know, or really understand how I feel," Chloe said, taking a large gulp of white wine. It was warm, and tasted stale.

She put the glass down quickly in case anyone noticed it was nearly empty, and insisted she have another one. Not wishing to be the centre of attention. Or to have people looking at her before realising that Natalie was, and she said the first thing that came to her. "I feel guilty talking about Jack behind his back."

"You find it difficult to talk about a lot of things," Natalie said, shaking her head, and wishing that she knew what was bothering Chloe. A stray thought popped into her mind, but what had happened to Daisy was a long time ago. It couldn't be worrying her sister after all this time. Natalie dismissed it. Only to think about Daisy again, later on.

CHAPTER 10

Jealousy And Arguments

Four weeks later, Mark still wasn't sure how he felt about Jack. Except that Chloe's husband was the sort of man he would have liked to be. The problem was it had taken Mark a long time to get over the taunting; punches, and bullying he had gone through at secondary school. Gradually however he was putting the past behind him, and could feel a sense of pride in what he had achieved. His job at Jenkins & Co played a large part in this, for which he was thankful. Building up his fitness and strength in the gym had also helped, and having good friends like Jamie. Being able to talk to him when he felt really low.

Before Chloe came along, Mark had started to believe that he did come across as someone who was successful. Nevertheless the past had left him with the niggling suspicion that he would never have the same charisma as Jack. He attributed this failing to the other deeply held belief he had about himself: He simply wasn't a success in love. However hard he tried.

As it was almost Spring, the weather was getting better and the housing market had picked up. There were a lot more properties on the company's books. Again, much to Mark's surprise, Chloe was excelling at making sales.

He told himself that he shouldn't be jealous, but that was easier said than done. After only being with Jenkins & Co for a few weeks, and not having any experience before that, she was taking the limelight away from him.

Mark raised himself up to his full height, without thinking about what he was doing. The way Mr Jones had spoken to her at their last office meeting had crossed his mind again. Chloe had been given the praise which, as far as Mark was concerned, was rightly his. Complaining about it later to Hannah, he couldn't resist saying how unfair he thought it was. Reminding her that he had been with the company the longest. He remembered Hannah glancing at him sympathetically when Mr Jones was in full flow. Although he wasn't sure if it had been one of her I told you so moments. It was impossible to tell, with Hannah. At least he couldn't, and which he had sometimes thought was why they found a lot to argue about.

Mark was distracted by his muscles aching, from the session he had this morning in the gym. He had been bench pressing, but adding an extra two and a half kilograms of weight to the bar had been his downfall. It was too heavy for him to lift. Scott, who was spotting him, didn't say anything. Just intervened so that the weights didn't fall onto his chest, and the others hadn't noticed. He was glad that he didn't have to suffer any comments made at his expense. He had quickly removed the plates, and lifted the eighty kilograms he knew that he could.

It didn't matter how long he thought about it, he still didn't know what he was going to do about Chloe, but something had to be done. To put a stop to her being thought of as the best salesperson in the office! Hannah had said she would think of something, which made him feel better. She was good at getting her own back, and why should someone like Chloe be in line for a bigger bonus than he was?

He still hadn't forgotten how she had turned down his invitation to the gym. Pretending that he had also invited Jack when he obviously hadn't. Or how much it had hurt his pride. He had started to change his mind about her after that. Listening to the names Hannah called her behind her back had made him realise Chloe did think she was better than everyone else. With her loud, know it all voice. He had told himself on a number of occasions that he didn't really fancy her any more. Except that he usually had to admit later this was a lie. When he was on his own in the evening. With only his computer for video games, and female company.

Meanwhile Chloe didn't realise Mark felt this way about her success at work. Although she instinctively sensed Hannah's ongoing dislike, she was totally oblivious to his jealousy. Her only concern was getting the sale and purchase of as many properties as she could, as quickly as possible. By doing her best to talk to the clients in a friendly, and professional manner; persuade them to sign the paperwork, and pay the deposit. She had even become used to talking to the solicitors dealing with the conveyancing transactions, and the other estate agents acting for the seller or buyer. The longer she had been in the office the easier it had become.

However, talking about it afterwards with Natalie, she realised that it was always only going to be a matter of time before there would be a confrontation with Mark. The inevitable occurred after he had taken several potential buyers to see a cottage in Waterfall Lane. Whilst the only one Chloe had taken to view the property came into the office the following day to buy it. As a result she was entitled to the commission once everything had been finalised, and Mark was furious. Causing him to do something which he had never done before. Even when Hannah had in the past taken their friendship a step too far, and been more annoying than usual.

He deliberately walked across the office to Chloe's desk, and told her exactly what he thought of her. At first, much to Hannah's delight. Shouting about how much he disliked false people, he accused her of having wheedled her way into the office. Getting them to teach her how to do something she wasn't qualified to. As if that wasn't enough, she had now stolen money from them. The commission on the Waterfall Lane sale belonged to him. Not her! His grand finale was banging the desk with his fist, and saying that he hoped she wouldn't be with them for much longer because she really ought to go.

When Chloe began to cry, Hannah was speechless and very impressed. She couldn't believe Mark had done it. Something she had wanted to do for a long time. Without being brave enough. Nevertheless when Sarah ran out of Mr Jones' office to intervene, she had to admit that he may have gone too far this time. It could easily lead to a disciplinary, and Sarah told him that he was to go into the office straight away. Hannah had never seen her look so angry, as she kept her arm around Chloe's shoulders. There was obviously no room for argument. Not this time.

Realising then that he may well have gone too far, Mark looked shame-faced, and mumbled an apology to Chloe when he walked past her desk on his way to the back room. Hannah smirked as she stood up, to get a glass of water for her. Although this seemed on the face of it to be a gesture of kindness, she intended it to be a show of support for Mark. That his verbal assault had never meant to be taken seriously, and Chloe needed to calm down after she had overreacted. At least that was what she was going to say, if Mr Jones or Sarah asked her about it.

She still believed Chloe had deserved every word of it, especially since her birthday. Chloe's attitude had become even worse after that. Insisting that Hannah get her this, or that, in the loud voice Mark and her hated. She had made it really difficult to get away with anything! Criticising the coffee for not being made how she liked it, so that it had to be done again. Mark was the only one who understood, and in Hannah's opinion, Chloe was treating him now in the same way.

Chloe took the glass of water from Hannah, without looking at her. She was also partially responsible for this. It was impossible to forget the way she had flirted with Jack, and how much they had both seemed to enjoy it. Nothing Hannah did was harmless fun, as far as Chloe was concerned. On top of everything else, she had started to get anxious about Jack leaving her. Every time she looked at Hannah she could see her flirting with him, and things hadn't gone well with Jack since then. They had been keeping their distance from each other. Whilst this might not have been apparent to anyone else, Chloe knew that Jack had withdrawn from her.

Even worse than that, she had done something which she never thought she would. She had searched through the messages on his mobile phone last night. He used her name as the password, so it was easy. Not really expecting to find anything, since he usually deleted messages as soon as he had read them, Chloe was horrified to find one from someone called Alice. He had agreed to meet her in a couple of days' time, at her house. She had reminded him that they were also meeting the following week, and the text ended with a big kiss.

Thankfully the water had still been running in the shower. So Jack didn't know what she had done, or that she now knew about Alice. Chloe sobbed even harder into her hands. As she remembered how she had felt seeing the text. She had dropped the phone onto the floor next to their bed, and burst into tears. Then knowing she had to stay in control of what may or may not be happening, she was propped up on her side of their bed with several pillows behind her, by the time Jack came out of the bathroom. Making it appear as if she had been reading a book, and nothing was wrong. Nevertheless it had been too difficult to keep up the pretence at work. When even Mark no longer seemed to like her, and all she had done was try to please everyone else.

Sarah was looking at her with concern. Wondering what was really behind all of this. Chloe didn't strike her as someone who would be daunted by Mark getting stressed and saying what he thought, but then she didn't really know a lot about her. Except that it hadn't of course been very long since she lost her father. Admittedly Mark was at fault. He did have a bit of a temper, and the job could get on top of anyone after a while. She could hear Mr Jones' raised voice behind the closed door of the office. Despite it being necessary for him to speak to Mark, she hoped that he wouldn't be too hard on him. Mark had his own difficulties. Sarah knew all about them from his mother, whom she had been at school with. Also Mr Jones' wife, and him. Although the manager had asked her not to mention this to anyone at work.

At least Chloe was married to Jack who was very nice. He seemed to dote on her. Despite Hannah trying to meddle, and now Mark today. They were quite a pair, she couldn't help thinking! It wasn't necessarily for the best when they were together. Sarah sighed, squeezing Chloe's shoulders. Glad that her breathing seemed to have returned to normal, after she had taken several sips of cold water. "That's better," she said, letting her arm fall away from Chloe's shoulders. "Don't worry about Mark! Mr Jones will deal with it. He shouldn't have spoken to you like that. You are doing exceptionally well, Chloe. You mustn't let office politics stop you from carrying on doing more of the same."

Chloe gave her a watery smile, and Sarah answered it with one of her own. It looked as if everything would soon blow over, and they could get on quietly with the rest of the day. Hopefully, without human resources having to be involved. She sometimes felt like she was managing a creche. Even as far as Graham Jones was concerned. She assumed that their shared childhood was the reason he thought he could get away with leaving most of the running the office to her, and spending his time in the back room. Although she had absolutely no idea what he did. He didn't seem to do a lot about getting new properties onto their books, or making any sales of his own. At least Mark was reasonably good at that, and Chloe had by now turned back to her computer. It wouldn't do Mark any harm at all to have some competition. If Chloe's predecessors had turned out better, this would probably have happened before now.

Meanwhile Chloe was wondering as she typed, how she would be able to keep this up. Despite the promises she had made, she was feeling completely exhausted, and more than a little overwhelmed by the sheer amount she had to learn very quickly. Also the strong personalities at home, and work. Falling out with Jack had been awful. The fear of losing him overwhelmed her again.

She had gone to two more sessions with Colin, to please Jack. Although she had insisted on going to them alone, and seeing Colin had filled her with dread. It was becoming increasingly difficult to hide behind the mask she had created, under the counsellor's skilful probing. She wished that she could tell Jack everything, but it was too late. He wouldn't understand. He would say that she should have shared it with him sooner. They had talked about not keeping secrets before they got married, and agreed to be completely honest with each other. Without her realising what might happen.

She couldn't kiss him goodnight after she had found the text from Alice, and he had insisted on knowing why. When she couldn't tell him, he had slept on the settee. Until he relented after a couple of hours, and crept into bed. Making the excuse that he had a stiff neck, and wouldn't be able to paint in the morning if it carried on. He had fallen asleep, with his back turned to her.

Chloe knew by then that she loved him too much, to wish that she hadn't married him. ...Whatever he might have done.

CHAPTER 11

Natalie Tries To Help Chloe

The Old Tavern wine bar, which had recently opened in a side street near the office, was almost empty when Chloe arrived. She waved to Natalie who had chosen a table near the fire.

She had offered to lock up, to make sure she was the last to leave, and the others wouldn't invite themselves for a drink. Mark had been wary of her since his outburst, and subsequent conversation with Mr Jones. She felt now as if she was walking on eggshells around him, but she had still been half-afraid that he would offer to stay behind. Until she was ready to leave. Taking every opportunity he could to overcompensate for his bad behaviour. Making Chloe feel suffocated by all the attention. She was delighted when she eventually overheard him mentioning to Hannah that he was going out with Jamie tonight, so would be leaving on time.

Natalie had been reading, and Chloe asked if she would like another drink as her glass was almost empty. When she brought two more wine glasses back to the table, she slipped her coat off and sat down. "Thank you for suggesting this," she said, sipping from her glass. Not expecting to drink too much as Natalie would be driving home.

"It's nice to get out of the apartment, especially during the week."

Natalie couldn't help noticing how tired, and drawn her sister looked. The bright red lipstick she was wearing drew attention to how pale she was. Creating a peculiar ghostly effect in the dimly lit wine bar. Chloe didn't look at all well, and since Natalie didn't really like the colour, she decided not to mention it.

She launched straight away instead into the reason for inviting Chloe. "I'm so glad you could come. I have been blaming myself for not being a better sister. I want us to be a lot closer than we have been, Chloe. I think Dad would have liked that, and it's long overdue. You can always come to me, if you need help with anything at all. Or even just to get out of the apartment for a drink, and a chat. Things don't have to change, now that you are married."

Chloe laughed lightly, trying to hide her embarrassment. What was Natalie talking about? Of course everything had changed, and not all of it for the better. Dad had died!

Natalie however knew her sister better than she thought, and leaned further across the table to say, "I have noticed that something is wrong, apart from us losing Dad. It isn't Jack, is it?"

Chloe glanced around the bar, worried about being overheard. Even though there were only three other people sitting at one of the tables on the opposite side of the room. "It's complicated, but Jack is part of the problem. I miss Dad too. I wish I could talk to him, and he could see that I am getting on well with the job." She hesitated.

"I should have got a better job a long time ago. He was proud of you becoming a teacher, and Harry doing well in the Navy. I should have tried harder. After all he did for us when Mum, and Gran died."

Natalie's heart sank. Getting closer to Chloe was going to be much more difficult than she had envisaged. "You mustn't think that! Dad and you had a special bond," she said, feeling frustrated that Chloe couldn't see what she was doing to herself. "I don't know why you should be so anxious about all this, or hard on yourself now. All of us have different lives. You are clever, Chloe, and a wonderful person. I always thought you would get yourself a better paid job once you were ready, if you wanted one. Don't forget what you have already achieved. Not everyone gets a University degree."

Natalie sipped her wine, thoughtfully. "I have seen too much of this at school. Students who believe that they have failed in some way. Parents trying to push their children before they are ready. Or who don't want to follow a particular academic path mum or dad is keen on. All of us have the potential to shine in our own way, at the right time. Dad knew that you were on the path to being who you wanted to be. He may have given you a little push into getting the estate agent's job, but that didn't mean he was disappointed in you earlier.

Chloe, you have to look instead at where you are now. You like what you do, and are succeeding at something new. I am very proud of you. As I know Mum and Dad would have been. Why not think of it, something along the lines of Dad always knew you had more in you to give, when the time was right?"

Natalie sighed, and squeezed her sister's hand. "You have done more than enough, and kept the promise you made to him. There isn't any need for regrets now, or wishing things had been different." Natalie hesitated, wondering whether she ought to say what she was thinking, and decided to after all. "As much as I would also give anything to hear his voice again and talk to him, we can't bring him back."

Without realising that the mask Chloe had created for herself was still firmly in place, hiding her thoughts, Natalie asked cautiously how Jack was. Without wishing to appear too interested in him, and make her sister feel jealous again.

"Oh, I don't know. I can't help thinking about how he was with Hannah. He never seems to laugh like that with me any more!" Chloe said, bitterly, causing Natalie to groan inwardly.

"Chloe, you have to trust him! You of all people should know how destructive jealousy can be," she said, as Daisy flitted through her mind and she tried to blank the image of the young woman's face from it. "All of us are attracted to other people. I'm not saying that there is an attraction between Jack and Hannah, but if there was it's normal and healthy. As long as they don't step over the line. So far as I know Jack has never done that, or given you any reason to doubt him."

When Chloe's face remained expressionless Natalie began to lose her temper, and she said, "go on, admit it!

Jack has never been unfaithful to you, or given you any real reason to think he might have been. So all these doubts you are having are totally unnecessary."

"What about Daisy?" Chloe replied, in a hard tone of voice.

"For goodness sake, that happened before the two of you got together. Even if Jack had been interested when she offered herself to him, in any way he wanted to have her, he didn't take her up on it. You have to stop this, Chloe. It's not doing you any good." Natalie paused, before continuing, gently. "Let Jack go with you to the next counselling session. I think it'll help."

Chloe appeared to be ignoring what she had said, and picked up her glass again, so Natalie tried to change the subject. To steer the conversation into what she thought might be calmer waters. "How are you getting on now with the meditation, and exercises Colin suggested you do?" she asked.

Chloe groaned. " Not very well at all. It's something else Jack is fed up about. I know he thinks I'm lazy, but the truth is I'm too tired to start doing yoga after work or close my eyes meditating. I fell asleep when I did it the second time. I had no idea what I was thinking about when I woke up. It's really hectic in the office, Nat. I find it difficult to switch off after having to pretend all day to be an extrovert, like everyone else. I'm just tired out, that's all."

"Amber, one of the teachers at school, is into things like this and she suggested a while ago that I try meditation. It really helped her to relax. She's always so calm with the kids. Not like me. They soon get me flustered!" Natalie smiled, pleased that Chloe seemed interested now in what she was saying. "Amber told me to think of my favourite flower. To imagine I was walking through the petals, and a wonderful perfume. Naturally I chose roses, but I couldn't decide which colour. So I tried doing it with different ones. Pink seemed to work best. It's amazing what you can come across when you are miles away. The secret is to breathe deeply, and slowly, focusing on every single breath. Release it, and relax. You are right though. It is easy to fall asleep doing it!"

Natalie tried to sound reassuring. While also not mentioning to Chloe that she had been thinking about changing her job for something less stressful. As she didn't know what that might be, and hadn't completely decided to make the change, she wanted to keep it to herself for the time being. Apart from telling Amber who had admitted in return, as they were talking confidentially, that she was a little scared of retiring. It would be the next step for her in a couple of years. She had absolutely no idea how she would fill her time. She didn't have any children or grandchildren; her partner had left her four years ago, and she didn't really have any hobbies. Not even a cat or dog. All of which had surprised Natalie. It crossed her mind then that you think you know someone, but it's almost impossible to be certain. Anything at all can be going through their thoughts.

"I've been thinking about you a lot, Chloe. We have had to cope with so much death in our lives. A lot of people don't have to face up to it until they are a lot older, and we were very young when Mum passed away. Not ready for it.

No wonder we cling to people now, and get jealous when we are afraid they might leave us! I'm going to admit it, as awful as it is. I'm a bit like that with Harry. I always feel down when he gets into a serious relationship, and I don't see him as much. He keeps trying to persuade me to find someone, but I don't seem to have been very lucky in meeting the right man," she said, sadly. "When I think about that I get scared of him leaving me, before he has even got here. I guess being scared is the main reason I have stayed single."

She looked at Chloe, and said, earnestly, "what are we like? Both of us are still holding onto Mum and Dad. While you are feeling anxious now about Jack." Natalie didn't add that these had also been Amber's thoughts on the matter when they had discussed it recently.

"I don't know, but maybe I got to know Mum a bit better than you did. Since I was older. She was in my life longer, and we talked about all sorts of things. I have been wondering if I took her death harder than I have done Dad's. While it's been the other way around for you. Gran protected you from a lot of what was going on at her funeral, and later. I can remember you asking over and over again where she was, and Gran making excuses about her having gone out, but they had to tell you in the end that she wouldn't be coming back. It took them a while to make you understand why. You became very quiet after that. Not saying a lot.

I know Mum believed in the power of love, Chloe. She told Harry and me never to forget how important it was. We were left a lot more to our own devices after she went, again because we were that bit older than you. Not that I am complaining. It was a hard time for everyone, and worse when Gran was taken not long afterwards." Natalie squeezed Chloe's hand, again. "At least we still have each other. Harry and Jack too, of course. Try being kinder to yourself. It'll help you feel better. A bit of self-love, like a new bath oil or nail polish can work wonders. I know that it always makes me feel better," she said, smiling.

Chloe looked at her sister, realising for the first time how hard Natalie had tried to open her heart to her, and she burst into tears. Unable to keep up the pretence any longer of being fully in control, she cried properly for the loss of their father. Along with the other deaths there had been across the years. Completely oblivious to her surroundings, and the curious glances she was attracting from the other customers.

When Natalie began to cry quietly and moved to sit next to her, they clung to each other. Until Chloe burst out laughing, after seeing how red her sister's face was in the mirror hanging on the opposite wall. Natalie soon joined in, feeling unable to cry any more, and they stared at each other in the mirror. Embarrassed that the young barman was by this time staring at them, clearly fascinated. As it went through his mind that they must have both lost their boyfriends.

"Seriously, Chloe," Natalie said, after she had blown her nose. "We need to stick together, and be strong to get through this. Also let other people help us. Not shut them out. I'm as bad as you are for doing that," she added, thinking it would make her sister feel better if she said it.

"Colin needs to know everything that has happened. Even about Daisy. You have to tell Jack too. He'll come around. All you are doing at the moment is pushing him away. Dad wouldn't have wanted that." She said the last few words as firmly as she could. Believing they were true.

Chloe stared at Natalie, and wondered if she could do what her sister was asking. As it seemed impossible. When Natalie smiled encouragingly however, she said, "okay, I'll try. I'll do my best to sort it out." Mentally adding this to the promise she had made earlier to her father.

Then completely out of the blue, Chloe also said, "Natalie, I want you to follow Jack!"

CHAPTER 12

What About Daisy?

Natalie tried to crouch down even lower than she was already doing. It hadn't been part of her plan, to hide behind the hedge on the opposite side of the road to the house Jack was visiting. She hadn't however been able to see the woman who let him in the first time he arrived, and he had closed the front door when he left an hour later. Calling goodbye over his shoulder.

Chloe had made such a fuss about this, that Natalie soon agreed to try one last time to see who the woman was. Having also become a little curious herself about what Jack was up to. Although she still thought that there was nothing to worry about, Chloe's anxiety seemed to be getting worse. Not better. As she hoped it would, after their conversation in the wine bar. Whatever Jack might be doing, the rift between Chloe and him appeared to have grown wider. At least her sister had said that he could go with her to see Colin next time, and Natalie had insisted she keep this promise. However her spying on him might turn out. Threatening Chloe that she would get Harry involved, if she didn't keep her side of the bargain.

The truth was Natalie had begun to feel overwhelmed by what was going on, so soon after the death of their father, and the problems she had at work. The cracks had also started to appear in her own life. Something would definitely have to change. A new job seemed to be the best option so far, she thought, as she glanced around at her surroundings. Thankfully it was a quiet street, and no one appeared to be at home in the neighbouring property. As she began peering through the hole in the fence at the house on the opposite of the road. Waiting for Jack to come along when he said he would, in the text Chloe had found on his phone.

After another five minutes which seemed to Natalie like a lifetime, and her knees were beginning to object to her crouching down, Jack turned the corner of the street and sauntered towards the house. Making Natalie feel as if she was standing naked behind a fence which was no longer there, and that he must surely be able to see her. Nevertheless he walked straight past the fence and her, to knock loudly on the front door. An elderly woman in a wheelchair opened it, and held it wide open. While Natalie took photographs of her, and them both. To show to Chloe later. She had thought about doing this earlier, to avoid her sister insisting that she come back again to obtain the proof!

It was easy to overhear their conversation. Jack had come to give her a painting lesson. She told him that she had set everything up on the table in the front room; bought some new watercolours that were lovely, and the cake she knew he liked for when they had a cup of tea.

At that point Natalie felt ashamed of Chloe, and herself. Is this what they had been reduced to, she thought with disgust? Wondered again what on earth she was doing here, and how she had let herself be persuaded to do something as crazy as this. Jack was a good man, one of the best. While Chloe had begged, and pleaded with her to follow him. Once Natalie had seen the anguish in her eyes she hadn't felt able to refuse. Following Jack seemed to be the only way to put an end to her sister's fear, and anxiety. The joy of having a younger sister whom you loved dearly, she thought bitterly to herself, and that all of this really had gotten out of hand. She hadn't believed that Jack, for whom admittedly she did have a soft spot, was cheating. She was more inclined now to agree with him that Chloe was ill. Her sister had even said, in that awful loud voice she used now and the brittle laugh, that she had considered instructing an enquiry agent but this seemed a bit too sordid.

Natalie crept out of the neighbour's front garden, hoping that no one would see her, and ask what she was doing. Also feeling more than a little sick at her part in the deception. She knew by then she had to put an end to what was going on, and had allowed herself to get dragged into. She would have to tell Jack, however badly he reacted, and make him see she didn't think she had a choice about following him. Hoping again, that when he had calmed down he would forgive her, and somehow be able to use what she told him to help Chloe.

Natalie sighed heavily. She had always been the peacemaker in the family, according to Dad. Especially after Mum's death, and wasn't that exactly what she was doing here? A tear slid down her cheek as she hurriedly walked away, and she brushed it away in irritation. She couldn't start feeling sorry for herself now. She would have to accept the consequence of her actions, if anyone had seen her behind the fence. She wasn't the only one who could take a photograph on a mobile phone.

Admittedly she would never have been able to forgive herself if Chloe had been right about Jack, and she hadn't helped her sister, but the whole thing was ludicrous. Dad would have been furious if he had known, and Natalie's heart was hammering hard now inside her chest, as she walked quickly away. Until she was almost running, and had to stop for a moment to catch her breath.

After she had bought herself a coffee and found a quiet table in the corner of one of the cafes on the High Street, where she could get a signal on her phone, she forwarded the photographs she had taken to Chloe's mobile. Intending to call her in a couple of minutes, but her sister rang her as soon as she had looked quickly at them. Natalie tried her best to tell Chloe how she felt, and believed it wasn't the right thing to have done. Whilst reluctantly admitting that she could understand why Chloe had asked her to do it. It was only right that Chloe should talk to Jack now about her fears, and tell him exactly how she felt.

However, as Natalie had anticipated, Chloe took the matter lightly and accused her sister of overreacting. It was clear that she had no intention whatsoever of talking to Jack. Insisting that it was perfectly normal for her to want to know what he was up to. He was her husband, so she had every right to check. Now that it is nothing, she obviously didn't need to do anything about it.

Natalie realised then that this was how Chloe dealt with anything that might be bothering her. Bottling it up inside, to hide the truth and how she really felt. Not only about Daisy! When Chloe went on to say that the photographs didn't actually prove Jack wasn't cheating, since there was still Hannah, any doubts Natalie might have had about telling her brother-in-law what had happened disappeared.

Feeling completely overwhelmed by this time, she decided not to wait but to call at the apartment. To get the conversation over and done with, before she had the chance to change her mind. She didn't trust calling him or sending a text in case Chloe searched his phone again. So after drinking the rest of her coffee, and checking that enough time had elapsed for the painting lesson and Jack to walk home again, she left the cafe with a heavy heart. Walking slowly to the apartment, as she tried to decide how to even begin repeating something as awful as this. Finally reaching the conclusion that she would have to tell him everything. Starting from the beginning. As Chloe definitely wouldn't do it herself. Possibly because she couldn't.

Needless to say Jack was shocked, and more than a little horrified, when Natalie explained what had happened. He almost couldn't believe it at first, and laughed. Thinking Chloe and her were playing a prank. Until Natalie showed him the photographs on her phone, and said repeatedly how sorry she was.

When Jack saw the stricken look on her face, he admitted that he had also reached the point of not being able to handle what was going on. It was far beyond anything he had gone through in the past, and what had happened to Chloe? The woman he loved, and had married. His voice had broken then, before he quickly pulled himself together. Seeing how much all of this had hurt Natalie, and what it must have taken for her to confess. He confided in her that Chloe's behaviour had unsettled him to such an extent that he was finding it hard to focus. He hadn't been getting any new ideas on what to paint, so had started to believe that the future he had been trying to create for them both might not be possible after all. He couldn't talk to Chloe about it. There wasn't any point in trying. She wouldn't listen. She was completely wrapt up in her job. Always excited, and glowing when she talked about it. Without realising just how odd she sounded. It wasn't right, and the worst part of this was, he didn't have a clue what to do next.

Natalie took a deep breath. It was time for her to tell Jack what had happened to Daisy. There was a good chance that it was still affecting Chloe, and from what Amber told her about the cognitive behavioural therapy she had undergone years ago, the treatment wouldn't work properly unless everything was out in the open.

Natalie looked at Jack, and knew that she had to choose between hurting him or helping her sister. When she cared about them both.

CHAPTER 13

A Matter Of Survival

After talking to Natalie Chloe couldn't help feeling tearful when she thought about their father. As this could become a problem at work she decided to distance herself from the other members of staff as much as possible, until she felt more able to cope, but it was proving difficult to do. Since powering through everything earlier was the only way she had been able to carry on.

Hannah and Mark had noticed the difference in her, and how she had calmed down. "Chloe's not in my face so much," Hannah said, with relief. "I guess she's leaving you alone too, my Superhero! After what you said to her." Blowing Mark a kiss.

Unsure whether or not she meant it, he blushed. It could equally have been her way of making fun of him. Hannah confused him a lot, and he would have been surprised to learn that she didn't really know what she was doing.

"Give it a rest, Hannah," he replied, believing that this would be the best way to deal with her. "You are tempting fate. Chloe could start being insufferable again, at any time. I shouldn't have lost it with her, but I am pleased to see how it turned out."

"I have absolutely no idea how you two find so much to talk about, and frankly, I don't want to know. Will you please get on with your work?" Mr Jones bellowed across the office at them. While Chloe and Sarah kept their eyes firmly on their computers. Neither Mark nor Hannah seemed perturbed however by getting another telling off. Both of them said, meekly and almost in unison, "yes, Mr Jones. Sorry!"

When the manager had returned to his office, Hannah poked Mark in the back with the handle of the sweeping brush, which the cleaner had left behind her desk last night. She knew as soon as she saw it, how useful it would be for doing this.

"What are you doing now?" Mark said in a loud voice, without intending to, as he turned around to glare at her. He didn't particularly want to get into any more trouble, after receiving a verbal warning for the way he had spoken to Chloe. Although Hannah and the others weren't aware that this had been the outcome of the episode. After Mr Jones decided to mention it to human resources and was told to do it.

"Nothing, my hero. Lighten up!" She said, grinning at him. As she dropped the broom stick onto the floor in case Mr Jones came out again unexpectedly. Her face fell unexpectedly, and she became serious. "You try too hard, Mark. Just be yourself. You would feel a lot happier, and do you know what? I would think you were really cool!"

After he turned back to his desk, Mark realised that he understood Hannah even less than he thought he did. Her moods were unpredictable at the best of times. Despite the sweeping brush incident, she wasn't her usual brash self this morning, and he asked her if she was okay the first opportunity he got.

"Yeah, I'm fine, thanks," she said, not intending at first to say any more but changed her mind. It would be good to talk about how she felt for a change. "It's just a bit difficult at home. Mum isn't well again, and Ryan is still playing up. I know she's worried about him, but he won't listen when I try to get him to behave."

Mark raised himself up so that he was no longer slouching in his chair. "If you need me to come and have a word with him, you only have to say," he replied, without seeing the look of horror on Hannah's face. She knew Mark was only trying to be kind, which touched the soft spot in her heart, but he wouldn't come off very well in a fight with her brother who was a lot more streetwise than him.

"Thank you," she said, again. "I'll bear that in mind, but things will settle down soon. They usually do."

"Are you still playing Fortnite?" he asked her then, hoping she would say yes. He was getting tired of spending so much time on his own. When she said that she was, he took the opportunity to add that he would see her online later tonight. Wondering afterwards if this might be a date. Since he couldn't decide if it was, he decided to ask Jamie. Asking for a friend, of course.

Meanwhile Chloe wasn't looking forward to leaving work early for her next appointment with Colin. She had intended to keep her promise to Natalie, at least at first, but then changed her mind. Even though breaking her promise was still worrying her, it would have meant exploring things she had been hiding for a long time. Not only from other people, but herself. Also breaking another promise she had made earlier to her Dad. She was doubtful too that talking about the past would help, but a small voice somewhere deep within her said that she had to do something. Things had changed between Natalie, and her. While Jack was really fed up. He didn't even seem interested in sex any more!

Natalie was adamant that he hadn't seen her following him, so that couldn't be the reason why he was being so cold and distant. Her sister would never tell him that Chloe had persuaded her to do it. Would she? If she had invited Jack to come to the meeting, as Natalie wanted her to, he would have found out about that and everything else he didn't know. Especially if she also told Colin about it.

Chloe was finding it difficult now to get beyond the enormity of what she had done. In the end it was easier to break her promise to Natalie, and not tell Jack about the appointment after all. Nor did she know whether she would be able to tell Colin everything, and break the promise she had made a long time ago to her Dad. A low sob escaped from her lips which she quickly managed to hide, in frustration at the software on her computer.

Little did she know that Jack was also worrying about the outcome of her next session with Colin. He was still reeling from the shock of what Natalie had told him. He felt very hurt by Chloe's lack of trust in him, and her astonishing ability to keep secrets, which he would never have thought her capable of. All that with Daisy had happened not long after Chloe and he got together, so why didn't she tell him?

After a lot of thought, and Chloe still not mentioning the appointment, he realised that she probably wasn't going to. If he had asked her about it, he guessed she would make some excuse so that he couldn't go with her. Since talking to the therapist was the only option they had left, as far as Jack could see, he decided to take matters into his own hands. He looked at the diary on her mobile phone when she was in the bedroom getting ready for work. Something he never thought he would do. With the result that they both arrived at the health centre at the same time. Too late to argue about him being there, since Colin was waiting by the window, and had seen them both arrive.

After saying hello and feeling the tension between them, Colin asked Chloe if she objected to Jack being present. She was about to say yes, when he interrupted her. Saying that it was vital he stayed, and he had only come to help. Not to argue, or cause trouble. There had been some developments which it was important Colin knew about. He would leave them to it afterwards, if this is what Chloe wanted, but he needed to speak to them both first.

Chloe's face was as white as a sheet by this time. Having guessed that Jack must know the truth, or at least some of it. Judging by the hard look on his face. Taking control of the situation as best as she could, she didn't reply. Only swept past them both, and took her usual seat in Colin's office. Soon to be joined by the two men.

Colin asked her if she wished to speak first, but not knowing what to say to keep control of the situation she shook her head. The headache she had at the office was still hammering at her temples, and she could feel her heart-beat thudding inside her chest. It felt as if the mask she had been wearing all this time was slipping from her face, and she didn't know how to put it back on. Whilst her heart was telling her that it was time to stop hiding the truth. She began to cry uncontrollably, and Colin passed the box of tissues to her before he made some tea. Using the kettle on the table in the corner of the room.

Jack looked at Chloe in despair, and an undisguised tenderness in his eyes. If only she had felt she could talk to him, and trusted him! He wished now that he was any-where, but here. Chloe couldn't even look at him, as the anguish he felt gnawed away inside him.

When Chloe was quiet again and sipping her tea, Jack told Colin that their marriage was disintegrating. She was still not talking to him about the things which worried her, and it had reached the point where she didn't trust him any more. There were also some things in her past which could well be affecting her anxiety levels now, but which so far as Jack knew, she hadn't mentioned.

"That's not true, Jack. I do trust you. I find it difficult to talk about the things which worry me, but that's always been the same. You are the extrovert in our marriage. Not me! You have also done some things I could complain about," Chloe said, indignantly. When Jack didn't reply immediately, she carried on speaking quickly.

He was surprised when she said, "why didn't you pass the phone to me after Harry called you, to say that Dad had passed away? He was my father! Yet, I had to be told about it second hand."

"Chloe, I can't believe you are still going on about that." Jack said, shaking his head. Until he realised that he ought to have known she would carry on trying to avoid revealing what she had kept hidden for so long, and talk about Daisy. Or even her need to ask Natalie to follow him. "I'm sorry you were upset. It didn't occur to me that you would be, but please stop trying to avoid the real issue now: Daisy! I know everything, Chloe, but you need to tell Colin what happened."

Colin decided he ought to intervene at this point, and he said, gently, "Chloe, can you tell us now who Daisy is, and what Jack is alluding to? He obviously felt it was important to come along today to ask you to talk about her."

When she didn't reply straight away, he told her to take her time. As Jack waited with bated breath, to find out why Chloe had done it.

CHAPTER 14

Anxiety Became Her Superpower

"It's all my fault. I am responsible for Dad's death, and Daisy's," Chloe said, in a monotone. "It was winter, and both of them died in car accidents."

She hesitated, surprised to feel a sense of relief that she could finally tell Jack, and her voice became stronger. "We were at a student party. I had been dragged along to it by the people on my course, and Daisy offered me a lift back to campus. I wasn't enjoying it, so I said yes. I didn't know her very well, but I thought I had seen her talking to Jack. She seemed nice, but as soon as we drove off she began to explain the real reason for offering me a lift. She wanted me to stop seeing you," Chloe said, looking at him.

"She said that you were her boyfriend. You loved each other, and she began describing how it was between you sexually. She had it all worked out. She told me you had slept together several times during freshers' week. She seemed to think this meant you were in a serious relationship. Dating at the very least. At first she said she understood what had happened, and would forgive me. Both of us knew what guys could be like for playing the field, and that you were just using me. I can still hear her voice, Jack. Taunting me!"

"How did that make you feel, Chloe?" Colin asked, seeing the hunted look in her eyes, and knew they were finally getting closer to the truth.

Chloe was staring into the distance, and seemed to be almost in a trance when she spoke. "We argued. She was adamant that I had to stop seeing you. She wouldn't believe me when I refused. She became angry. Calling me lots of horrible names. We were travelling along a road in the middle of nowhere. I wasn't sure where we were, and I was lucky that she had to slow down. It was snowing heavily. She was finding it hard to see through the windscreen. I remember thinking how dirty it looked. When she stopped the car to try to clear it, I opened the passenger door and got out. She shouted at me to stop, but I had already started to run towards the trees. Not knowing where I was going. Only that I had to get away from her. I was frightened of what she would do, Jack," Chloe's eyes pleaded with him, to understand.

"Daisy pulled back onto the road, too quickly. The ice slid her car into the opposite lane, spinning it directly in front of an articulated lorry. I saw everything! No one else was hurt except her, and the Police said that her bag had been thrown from the car. They found it later, with her journal inside. She hadn't mentioned you by name, Jack. Using a nickname instead, but I knew it was you. After the way she had talked about you. She called you,"her bear!" Chloe said, looking accusingly at Jack. Making him blush before she carried on.

"I was questioned by the Police, but I didn't tell them anything. I guess I was still too traumatised to say a lot.

Nat knew it was you, Jack. She guessed, and Dad told me to keep out of it. He didn't want my name dragged through the newspapers unnecessarily, and at the Inquest. Later on he thought I might be in trouble for hiding my version of events from the Police, if anyone ever found out. So he swore all of us to secrecy: Nat; Harry, and me. I didn't believe that you were still seeing Daisy. I never thought you would find out about her and I arguing, or exactly how she had died."

She paused for a second. "Dad must have lost concentration when he was driving. He had been worrying about me, and the new job. Now I am losing you after going through all that, because of not being able to forget about it. As you can see, everything is all my fault!"

"I didn't know about you being in the car with Daisy. I remember you were away from Uni for three weeks," Jack said, anxiously. "You didn't answer my texts. After you had told me you were ill, and would see me again in the New Year. You kept everything vague. When you came back we just picked up where we had left off." He felt overwhelmed by Chloe's revelation. Natalie hadn't told him Steve had insisted they keep what had happened a secret, or that Chloe held herself responsible for both deaths. He thought she had only witnessed Daisy's death. He didn't realise how difficult Natalie had found it to tell him even this. How disloyal she felt to both her sister, and late father.

"In the end I couldn't bear thinking about that night, or the thought of talking to you about it. We were getting on so well I didn't want to risk anything spoiling it. I am not proud of what I did, Jack," Chloe said, with her head hung low. So that she wouldn't have to look at Colin, or him.

"When you asked me for a date, I couldn't believe at first that you were interested in someone like me. I had liked you for a long time. Everyone wanted to be with you, especially the girls. It was easy to fall in love with you, and I was just secretly starting to hope everything could work out when Daisy came along. I didn't know how to handle it, Jack! I wasn't sure if I should talk to someone else about it, but then who? It wasn't as if I had a lot of friends, vying with each other to be my best friend, and I hadn't seen or spoken to Natalie for a while. We didn't live in each other's pockets."

Chloe hesitated. Wishing she could look at him now, and that his arms were around her. She sighed heavily. "I suppose the longer I left it the more anxious I became about losing you." Her voice became stronger then. "As far as I am concerned Daisy's death was my fault. I was in the car with her that night. I watched it happen. If we hadn't been arguing she would have been more careful, and still be alive." She began to cry in earnest, as the memories of that night came flooding back to her in technicolour.

After a moment or two without looking at either Jack or Colin, she tried to dry her eyes and said, sadly. "Dad was only trying to help me when he didn't want anyone else to know I was in the car. He arranged a few counselling sessions with a friend of a friend, so I wouldn't have the stigma of it being on my medical records. It didn't do a lot of good. After Daisy died, and whatever Dad said, I knew that he still worried about me. When we had those deep conversations about me being able to cope, and how I should do it, I knew I was right.

Yes, I did promise to be successful and that's why I was so intent on being good at my job. Also to help you, Jack, which I really wanted to do. How could I make things even more complicated by talking about Daisy? Especially after Dad died, and I had told him I would never speak of the accident or her again. I missed the opportunity to tell my husband, and anyone else. For which I am deeply sorry." Chloe sobbed into her tissue, before she blew her nose.

"Had I been a bit nicer to both of them I honestly think none of this would have happened."

Jack's voice was also filled with sadness. Hearing Chloe speak about it for the first time, and that he had been at the heart of all this for so long. Leaving the woman he loved not knowing which way to turn, and ultimately making her ill. "Daisy lied, Chloe!" He said, firmly. "She couldn't bear the thought of anyone dumping her, and whatever she told you, I wouldn't have gone back to her. Even if you had told me our relationship was over. I would have spent a very long time trying to get you back, then never being over you completely if I couldn't fix it. Not run after Daisy! Some people are delusional, and she definitely was one of them. With the benefit of hindsight, she probably was a narcissist. Everything we did, or didn't do, had to be about her.

I feel devastated now that you couldn't share this with me. It was a huge relief once she was no longer in my life. That I didn't have to see her again or put up with her tears and tantrums. When she didn't get her own way. I don't like speaking ill of the dead," he said, glancing at Colin before he looked back at Chloe. "I am only saying this now because it's you I care about, Chloe. Not her."

Jack cleared his throat before he carried on. "According to Natalie, Harry intended to tell me first about your Dad's accident. So that I could give the bad news to you. Your family agreed that after what happened to Daisy, if you had to deal with another death, you wouldn't be told directly. It was to soften the blow. Since you had become overly upset, and anxious after her accident. Following your mother, and grandmother's passing.

Chloe smiled sadly at Jack. "It was a difficult time for everyone," she said. "It was the same at Dad's funeral as it was when Daisy died. I wanted to help by telling the truth. Everyone seemed to have so many questions about what had happened to her, but I couldn't say anything. Then I wasn't allowed to make any of the decisions about Dad's funeral. Harry and Natalie did all of it. Not only had I been responsible for two deaths, but I also felt excluded."

Conscious of the time passing quickly Colin broke the silence, after a couple of minutes of Chloe and Jack being deep in thought. "Thank you, both of you. However painful this might now seem, Chloe, I believe that you have made a huge step forward today. I can see now that you have been using the anxiety you suffered to protect yourself. I realised at our first session that you could well have underlying issues which needed to be resolved, but the effect bereavement has had on you runs much deeper than I thought."

Although it wasn't Colin's function as a counsellor to pass judgement on anything which had happened, he still couldn't help feeling that her father may well have been manipulative and controlling in the way he had acted. Causing Chloe to suffer unnecessarily. For his own reasons, of course. He had probably worried too much about raising a young family after his wife's death, and had also to deal with her bereavement.

Colin's concern now was solely to help Chloe find the best way to cope with this series of events, and be able to get on with her life which he hoped Jack would still be a part of. Unfortunately there weren't any guarantees of this. Jack had his own demons now to deal with. Given the sort of man he was, Colin thought he would more than likely be blaming himself for what had happened to Chloe earlier, leading up to Daisy's death. Even though there wasn't a valid reason for this.

"Chloe, you have gone through an enormous amount," he said, turning his attention back to her. "Even before your recent life changes; Moving house; getting married, and starting a new job in which you didn't have any previous experience. Thankfully we appear now to have got to the heart of the matter, and the very heavy burden of the secrets you have been carrying, if I may say so.

In my opinion you have been using your anxiety as a superpower. I am glad that made you smile. Even just a little bit. I am not talking about you joining the superheroes, but finding the best way to cope naturally with everything that has happened. Your Dad's passing pushed you finally into using your anxiety this way. So that you didn't have what might be described as a typical reaction to the grief you felt on his death. It is something very special, Chloe. Only a few percent of people do this when they suffer. Using their anxiety in a good way, to help themselves succeed, and get through the challenges they might still be facing.

Instead of being scared of the overwhelming feelings, things like grief can bring on, I believe that you have embraced the fight or flight response which your anxiety caused. Using its symptoms to your advantage. I hope that we can help you think about all this differently now. So that you no longer feel that what happened was your fault, and you shall find some peace."

Since Chloe was now looking at him, slightly puzzled by this, Colin explained it further. "Essentially what happens in the fight or flight response is that our hearts race to pump blood around our bodies a lot quicker, to get it to where we need it in the vital organs. Our breathing rate also increases to let in more oxygen. The heightened state of alertness; vivid vision, and almost supersonic hearing you have been experiencing were all part of this. Anxiety caused the bursts of energy you had, and I noticed that you began talking a lot faster. You were actually using this as a mask, to try to cover up what you were feeling subconsciously. All this is an important part of the body's survival response system, and symptoms like this typically occur when someone is in real danger.

Thankfully when we are dealing with an anxiety disorder now we aren't usually facing any real danger as such. In your case, Chloe, it was more than likely prompted by a buildup of excessive stress; the major life events you experienced, and of course your grief. Don't forget you got married; moved house, and started a new job. In many instances one major life event is enough to cause excessive stress, which can then develop into excessive anxiety. Making people more prone to panic attacks, and the development of anxiety disorders.

Until I learned about Daisy I had been wondering if the major life events you had been subjected to were the reason you reacted to your anxiety in the way you did, and this was purely speculative on my part. A lot of people when they first experience the intense symptoms of the fight or flight system become afraid of them. They start to worry about their heart racing; fixate on their heightened alertness, and may even begin to avoid situations where the anxiety could occur. Obviously having a detrimental impact on their lives. Your response, Chloe, was almost the opposite. In certain situations you subconsciously used the anxiety symptoms you had to your advantage."

Colin paused to catch his breath, and drink a mouthful of cold tea before he carried on speaking. "The important message to take away from all this is that even though your reaction to excessive anxiety was in the minority, Chloe, it was still important to recognise and treat it. While the symptoms might not be particularly scary to you, unlike other people, they can still be having a detrimental impact. It's important too, to separate the grief you have experienced as a result of your father's death, from this excessive anxiety. Treating them as two separate processes. I am going to suggest that you have further counselling sessions to explore the different stages of your grief, and there are things we can put in place to help support you. The stages can occur in any order, and there isn't a set timeline for them.

I will also make a plan to help you with your stress. As if we can manage to reduce this it should have an impact over time on your anxiety levels. Having more cognitive behavioural sessions should help you identify when you are feeling anxious; the sensations you are experiencing, and how you are likely to behave when these feelings occur. I will also let you have a few more self help resources, and work books, and we'll get you booked in for a review. As you can see there is plenty we can do to help you."

Chloe thanked Colin, after glancing at Jack, She was more worried about her husband than anything else. She had said, and done some awful things, since her father had died. Jack hadn't mentioned anything about her getting Natalie to follow him, but she guessed that he knew about it. Not trusting him would have hurt him badly. Not to mention done a lot of damage to their marriage. Why was life so unfair? They had hardly had any time together, as a married couple, before Dad died. She was on the point of losing both of them. As she wasn't sure now if Jack would want to try again. There might be too many bridges to mend.

How could she admit that she still thought of Daisy, every time she looked at him?

While Jack was also left wondering whether Chloe and he would be able to save their marriage. He sensed her hostility when she looked at him. Making him feel confused. He still loved her, and had only been trying to help her.

CHAPTER 15

Chloe And Jack

Both Chloe and Jack had left the counselling session feeling emotionally exhausted. He couldn't believe that Steve had told Chloe not to tell anyone what had really happened on the night Daisy died. However when he had calmed down he realised that her father had probably only been trying to protect her. Like he always did.

It was several weeks later, and Chloe had carried on seeing Colin Maitland. She knew it was the right time now for her to visit the cemetery. She hadn't been to her father's grave by herself, since the funeral. She was crying as she arranged the spring flowers she had brought with her. It was peaceful, the birds were singing, and Chloe knew that what she felt was grief.

She was allowed to miss her Dad; still be upset about his sudden death and as Colin had told her, deal with his loss in her own way. She was grateful to Colin now, and for all of the help he had given to her. He had somehow managed to arrange the extra sessions she needed, fairly quickly, after she had talked about Daisy. She suspected that he had stayed at the health centre later than usual to do it. Whilst she had been off work staying with Natalie.

Chloe turned her head quickly when she felt that some-one was watching her. Not wishing to be disturbed, she was shocked to see Jack standing on the path behind the gravestones. She hadn't seen him since the day after the Daisy counselling session, as she now called it in her thoughts, or when she talked to Colin about it. Jack had his hands in the pockets of his favourite jacket, and was looking awkward. Like he did, when he had something important to say.

Her heart went out to him. It was difficult to believe that they had gone through so much. The question now was whether it was going to make their marriage stronger, or lead to them breaking up. Chloe still didn't know the answer. Only what she would much prefer to do. She hadn't wanted to leave him when she went to stay with Natalie, but it seemed at the time to be the only option. Given how she felt after revealing everything she had hidden for so long. However the longer it had gone on for the more she began to doubt whether she had made the right decision.

They had spoken very little on the phone since that day, as it made her feel too anxious, and Jack had wanted her to stay. He said that he needed her with him. When all she could think about was clearing her head. Without feeling pressured to talk through everything again, until she was ready to do so. Nevertheless it was a risk she didn't think of at the outset, but her absence might have ended up pushing him further away. Chloe was afraid now that Jack might not want her back, and she assumed he had come here to tell her what he had decided.

He walked in what seemed like slow motion across the grass, to stand next to her while she finished arranging the flowers, and stood up. He took her arm then to help her, and she was grateful that he did. Even though she didn't need him to. "Come on," he said, quietly. "We need to talk."

Chloe followed him back onto the path, without saying anything. She was afraid to break the silence in case what he had to say wasn't what she wanted to hear, and she was surprised when he began talking about his painting. How he hadn't been able to carry on with his own work because of the way things had been between them. His voice faltered, and she squeezed his arm in the way she used to do before they were married. To give him time to collect his thoughts, and carry on.

He repeated what she already knew in that he couldn't bear to see how much she had changed after they moved to Mappingham, and she clearly hadn't been well. Knowing that he had to do something to help her relieve the pressure she was under, he decided to earn some extra money by giving painting lessons. It was what he had been doing when Natalie saw him going into Alice's house that day. The guilt about her working and earning money to support them both had been gnawing at him inside. Especially after he learned the truth about how much she had been suffering.

He had tried to make good use of the time they had been apart, and his voice was filled with sadness when he said this. Even though he smiled at her. He had also been teaching Margaret, a sprightly octogenarian, to paint and it had given her a new lease of life. Or at least that was what she said, and Jack, the idea of her asking her friends if anyone else would like to learn. He now had three other clients because of this, and was certain he could get more. He began talking then about Chloe being able to get another job, if she wanted one. Maybe the local florist could offer her one?

Although he didn't say that he had missed her, it did seem as if he wanted them to stay together. Chloe felt a weight lift from her shoulders, and a lightness within her. Happiness she supposed. Something she hadn't felt for a long time. When she tried to show concern that teaching others was taking him away from his own painting, Jack said that he was happy doing it. He was still working with paints and a canvas, also helping other people. He told her that he liked his elderly clients, and didn't want to let them down. At least until he had taught them enough to have the confidence to carry on painting by themselves. Maybe then, just getting together with them once in a while.

Chloe already knew a lot of this from the Daisy counselling session he had attended, but she didn't say anything. It was Jack's way to talk around something, before he reached the most important part. "How did you know I would be here," she said, when it looked as if he was waiting for her to reply.

"I went to the office. I thought you would be back at work by now. I wanted to take you out for lunch, with my earnings," he said, shyly. "Also to tell you that I had sold a painting. Sam called, and Sarah told me where you had gone." He scrutinised her face. "She told me she had asked if you were okay, as you looked unhappy. I got four hundred pounds for it," he couldn't help adding proudly, and without being able to wait to tell her. Making the news slightly out of context.

Chloe smiled up at him, genuinely pleased at his success. "That's wonderful, Jack. You are a brilliant painter. I always believed that you could do it. Given the opportunity. I know it might not have seemed like it the last time I saw you with Colin, but I really appreciated what you did that day to help me. I also remember you didn't like the idea of giving lessons when you mentioned it a long time ago." She hesitated, wondering whether she should be the one to bring this up, or wait for him to say it. Jack seemed however to be at a loss for words now, and although Chloe didn't know this, he was terrified of saying the wrong thing.

"I couldn't talk to you about Daisy. The longer I left it the harder it seemed to do, and I was convinced that you would be annoyed with me for keeping secrets. It was such an awful thing to happen," she said, anxiously. "I know I've been foolish, Jack, and made a mess of everything. Colin has been helping me to come to terms with it. Thank goodness, Natalie had the sense to tell you or we wouldn't have been having this conversation." She smiled shyly at him.

"I knew Steve, and I liked him a lot. Chloe. Your Dad would have loved you whether or not you became an estate agent," he said, looking deeply into her eyes. "The same as me," he added, gently. You have still got me, if you want me." Hesitating for only a moment, he drew her into his arms, and she felt safe for the first time in a long time.

"Chloe, I love you very much. Please can we try again? I have missed you!" He kissed her tenderly then, and felt his heart respond when she didn't resist.

He had slept on the settee the night after the counselling session, and his world had fallen apart when she told him the following morning that she had decided to stay with Natalie. Trying to make light of it by saying at least she wouldn't have had to cope with his silence, and grunts, if she went. Nevertheless her eyes had betrayed the hurt she was feeling inside, but when he had tried to get her to stay she refused. Asking him to give her some time to sort herself out.

"I have one condition," he added, as Chloe's heart began to break all over again. "Hey, it's only that we start talking to each other from now on about how we feel, and what we are thinking. As much as I would like to believe that I have a mind reading superpower, I'm sure Colin wouldn't agree, and I don't really have one."

Jack's smile melted any doubts Chloe had left, and she knew that she had been right to carry on hoping this would happen. "Yes," she said, as her body melted into his arms which were already around her. They would have a chance after all, to get through this.

"Come on, it's freezing out here," Jack said, eventually as he rubbed his hands together. "Let's go for a glass of wine, and a sandwich. You have a rich husband, remember!"

Without knowing why it happened Hannah's face flitted across his, before Chloe could remove it from her thoughts. She smiled then, and slipped her arm through his. "I want the stool by the fire when you go to the bar to order the food," she told him.

"I don't know about that," he said, laughing. "Race you there!"

Chloe looked at Jack in disbelief as he suddenly began to run. Glad that she had worn low heeled boots, and that she could follow him.

Later that day he bought a dozen red roses for her from the money he had earned, and he cooked a seafood pasta for their supper. They couldn't usually afford to do this but, as Jack said, they had a lot to celebrate. They were back together, and they had both changed. Chloe seemed to be feeling less anxious, and had more sessions booked in with Colin. Whilst he felt in control again, Life no longer appeared to be pointless.

The seafood pasta and Chianti reminded him of those hot, summer, nights he spent in Italy. They had so much more to look forward to! He took Chloe's hand, and closed the bedroom door behind them. Without either of them knowing what the future would hold.

The End

Author Note

I hope you have enjoyed reading *Chloe*, the first book in the *Anxiety Superpower series*.

The series takes place in Mappingham, a fictitious town near London, but Chloe and Jack's story could have happened anywhere. I thought of the United States and other places when I was considering the setting, because of the sheer number of community members we have from around the world, for which I am very grateful. So it was a difficult choice, and in the end the best option seemed to be a fictitious town. As I am also from the UK I already knew how Chloe would get an appointment on our National Health Service; the way property is bought and sold here, and so on.

You'll find out more about what happens to Chloe and Jack in the other books in the series, and how the other characters and they go on to manage their anxiety levels.

Jack will be available shortly, as Book 2 in the series.

In the meantime, please download the new DLC Anxiety app in the Google Play Store or Apple Store. It's completely FREE, and is a great place to start talking about *Chloe* with the DLC community. You'll be very welcome to join us.

If you can spare a couple of minutes and you enjoyed the book, I would also love for you to leave a short review. It will help other readers find *Chloe*, and mean the world to me.

All the best,

Dean

PS. Hey! I can't leave you wondering what will happen next, without any idea of what that might be. So here's a short extract from *Jack* I hope you'll enjoy:

Jack and Chloe have left the apartment, and bought a cottage in Mappingham which they are renovating. Although she is still at Jenkins & Co she wants to get pregnant, and Jack is now a successful artist.

You might think at first glance that their lives sound amazing, but as you know, it's rarely that simple. Unfortunately, the cracks have reappeared in their relationship …

"I am sick and tired of it, Jack. Hannah is a trouble-maker, and you seem to think that the sun shines out of her. You only have to look at what she did to Mark, to see that I'm right!" Chloe said, glaring at him.

Jack groaned inwardly. He was tired, and all he wanted to do was watch the rest of the movie in peace. "You are exaggerating as usual, Chloe. All I did was talk to her," he said, trying to sound reasonable. As he rubbed his face, and knew full well that there had been a bit more to it than that.

Unable to sit next to him any longer on the old settee, which was one of the places where they used to make love, she stood up quickly. Leaving Jack staring at the television screen. She flounced up the stairs, and across the landing, to sit in her favourite place on the floor next to the bed. Wondering if he would sleep in his studio again tonight. He had been doing that a lot, lately.

Chloe frowned, when she felt the familiar pain in her temples, and her heart thudding inside her chest. Whatever Jack did, or didn't do, she had to try to calm down. To stop constantly thinking about Hannah and him. She didn't have anyone to talk to. Not even Natalie, and it was definitely back. Worse this time. Everything Colin Maitland told her was due to extreme anxiety, and stress.

Nevertheless it also presumably meant that she would be able to do it, before the baby came. Her anxiety super-power would help her find out what Hannah was up to. When it was obvious that she wanted Jack!

A tear trickled down Chloe's face. This was her own fault. If only she hadn't agreed with him that they ought to have a party, after they moved in two years ago, none of this would have happened. She was certain of it, now.

I would love to hear what you think of this extract.

If you haven't already done so, please download the new DLC Anxiety app from the Google Play Store or Apple Store, to start talking about *Chloe* and *Jack* with the DLC Community and me.

Remember too that things may be as they seem, but sometimes they are not. Tantalising, isn't it? Not knowing,

and we'll have to leave this now to your imagination…
Until *Jack* is on Amazon.

When you can find out what really happened between Hannah and him, also to Mark, and of course Chloe.

I think you'll be surprised.

Warmly,

Dean